The Chosen Instrument

Love to Evie

Calvin.

Henry

Books by Henry Calvin

HENRY CALVIN

The Chosen Instrument

HUTCHINSON OF LONDON

HUTCHINSON & CO (*Publishers*) LTD
178–202 Great Portland Street, London W1

London Melbourne Sydney
Auckland Bombay Toronto
Johannesburg New York

First published 1969

*This book has been set in Fournier, printed in Great Britain
on Antique Wove paper by Anchor Press, and
bound by Wm. Brendon, both of Tiptree, Essex*

09 097190 6

THE airport building was small but quite decent, a long one-storey cedar prefab, with a big sign on the side facing the tarmac, WELCOME TO TATRA. The man at the Customs check probably hadn't read the sign, or perhaps Dai had put him off. Dai has a simple hatred of Customs men, immigration men, policemen, traffic wardens and anybody else who enjoys brief authority, and his hatred shows. When he said nothing to declare it sounded like an invitation to a razor fight. The Customs man opened his bag and started meticulously to shake out each garment, crumple it with skilled hands and dump it on the dusty counter.

I didn't say anything. If that's the only amusement a man can find, God help him. Dai didn't say anything, but I reckoned that the Customs man was two shirts away from being yanked across the counter and shaken toothless when Major Land arrived, and the little official shambled to a kind of attention and bobbed and cringed.

'Mr Carlyle? Sorry I am a little late.'

He put out his hand to shake mine, and I said, 'And Mr Owen.'

Dai thought about it for half a second before he accepted the major's handshake, but Land was already turning his attention to the Customs man and saying, quite genially, 'That is no way to treat honoured visitors.'

And the Customs man was grinning and cringing hideously and ramming stuff back in the bag and babbling: 'Routine, Major, I didn't know . . . the rules . . . sorry, sir.' The last word was to Dai, who scowled in reply.

Two scruffy porters appeared, to carry the bags through the building to a big Ford convertible. It had a pennant flying on the bonnet, but no chauffeur except the Major.

'Sir Malcolm also apologises,' he said amiably. 'He was suddenly involved in Cabinet discussions. But he will be free soon.' The Major put his foot down and the car roared forward with a cloud of incinerated rubber behind it. I was in front beside him. Dai had vaulted into the rear seat; maybe he didn't like majors very much either.

The Major was as handsome as hell, an inch or two taller than myself, brown face, black eyes, white teeth, and the uniform was de luxe Hollywood Ruritarian. I couldn't work out why Tatra had an army at all, with a population half the size of London's, but it was a long time since I had stopped thinking about politics and it was none of my business. At least he had learned to drive, probably at Monza from the way he threw the car round the bends in the lee of the mountains. The town was about eight miles from the airport, and we had gone five, in four minutes, when he looked up from the road and said 'Ah!'

Something like four tons of boulder was trundling down the mountainside on our left and ahead, and by my own calculations it was beautifully timed to arrive on the road two hundred yards ahead at exactly the same time as we did. We were doing seventy. Without relaxing his smile the Major went up to ninety. It was a moment for nice decisions. I suppose he might just have managed to slow down enough to stop short of the rockfall, but if he had he might still have had enough speed to crumple us against it. I twisted round and saw the great lump bouncing like a slow-motion tennis-ball across the road in our wake.

After that he stopped, and reversed violently.

'Do you get much of that?' I asked him. I was quaking. I must say it didn't look like a landslide formation; there were no obvious faults or big outcrops, and the slope was steep but not steep enough.

'Now and then.' He was still smiling as he slammed on the brake and I was flung against the seat.

The Major reached under the dashboard and jerked out a little automatic carbine. He twisted round in his seat, squinted at the rockface above on the left, and loosed a dozen rounds at it. The ricochets whanged and echoed away through the mountains and lost themselves, and the Major shrugged as if in apology, turned round and scanned the coastal plain on our right. In the heat shimmer I saw a couple of dozen goats, maybe four hundred yards away, and a man, or a boy, standing among them and holding his hand up against the sun glare. The Major made a little noise of pleasure in his throat and sighted along the carbine barrel at him, across the front of my chest. I pushed the barrel up to the sky as he fired. It was bloody hot. The man with the goats fell on his face and disappeared.

The Major said tck, paused, and then laughed.

'You are probably right,' he said. 'But if he didn't do it, at least he knew about it.'

'Do you pot a peasant every time there's a bloody landslide?' Dai asked from the rear seat. The Major was already clipping the carbine back in its place and accelerating forward.

'We have our little troubles,' he said happily. 'And our troublemakers.'

'And don't think you don't deserve them,' said Dai. I decided that Dai had added majors to his list.

'I am sorry,' said the Major, 'that you have had such an exciting introduction to Tatra. You will understand the situation better in a few days.' He was still smiling, but a trace of anger showed through. I couldn't tell whether it was because of the landslide or his failure to pot the peasant.

'And to think we could have been doing a nice sewage contract in Liverpool,' Dai said.

The Major laughed and said to me, 'I didn't mean to frighten your assistant.'

I wasn't going to say anything. Keep your mouth shut and do your job and keep out of trouble, I always think. But I couldn't resist it.

'You will be a very very old major before you ever frighten my friend,' I said.

'No no, honest I'm like a jelly,' Dai said. And we both laughed. The Major didn't quite get it. But I was even sorrier than Dai about the Liverpool sewage contract.

2

WE were booked in at the Louis, with a suite each on the ground floor, giving on to a little courtyard with a pool and a fountain. The place was old, probably Victorian, but it was cool and comfortable, and the plumbing worked. I had a bath and changed, and found Dai already in the yard, with a bottle of gin and a bucket of ice and a jug of lemonade, and we waited for Malcolm to call when he was finished with the Cabinet.

'Top-level stuff,' Dai said agreeably. 'My mam would whirl in her grave if she could see me working the badinage with the Cabinet advisers. And drinking gin in the middle of the day. Drinking anything any time. The corruption of the capitalist fleshpots,' he added in his mam's voice. 'If they can't beat you they'll buy you, boy, better die underground than sell out. Cheers, Mam.'

'If that boulder had hit us your mam would lie happy,' I said. I drank more gin than I usually did. I wasn't actually shaking, but my forearms felt weak in spite of conscious relaxation and deep breathing exercises in the bath.

'When you got to go you got to go,' he said. Dai never spent much energy looking back or ahead. 'You take life too serious, boss.'

'Don't call me boss.'

'It's a fact, innit? Never blink a fact, even if you want to change the world you got to accept it as it is first, Mam always said. If a mountain has your number on it it will fall on you. When do we start workin', then? Not that I'm in a hurry.' He pushed off one of his shoes and dipped his bare foot in the little pool.

He was doing that when Malcolm arrived, and he hastily pulled out the wet foot and tried to stuff it back in the shoe. Malcolm noticed all right, because I saw the flicker of a smile, but he didn't say anything except 'John! Good. Good good good to see you.' He put his hands on my shoulders and looked at me while Dai stood up squelching.

'And the famous Dai Owen,' Malcolm said.

Dai took his handshake and said, 'Most of it is a damnable lie, I never laid a finger on the barmaid.' Malcolm laughed and kept a hold of his hand while they candidly studied each other.

'All I've heard is good,' Malcolm told him, and Dai said: 'I know, he's been ravin' about you too.'

'*That's* a damnable lie, Malcolm,' I said. 'I've hardly mentioned you.'

'You don't have to put it in words, boy,' Dai said contemptuously. 'Will you have some gin, Sir Malcolm?'

Malcolm tutted and said, 'The sir's only for Sundays and strangers. No, thank you, Dai . . .' He turned to me and smiled. 'Still the pussyfoot, John, no vices at all except exploiting my friends.'

It was good to see him again, and Dai was being wicked when he said that I had raved about Malcolm. I'm always afraid of raving about a friend in case other friends expect a paragon and are disappointed. I was apprehensive about Dai's reaction to him, because with Dai you can never tell. But Dai seemed happy and impressed, and was pouring a glass of lemonade.

Malcolm was hardly changed in ten years. The touch of grey suited him. The same deep eyes behind the same heavy-rimmed glasses, and the same air of reassuring confidence. I had always felt that he must have been born fully grown. He sat down and we all sat down, and he turned serious and said, 'You had some trouble on the way from the airport, John.'

'A bit.' Merely meeting him again had calmed me down. I told him about the rockfall and he nodded while he listened.

'It's an odd little country,' he agreed. 'But you could probably live here for ten years and never see another sign of violence. Some of the hill people are still nomads. Quite childlike, it's fantastic in this day and age. When I hear about an incident like this I sometimes think they must be like the people in Golding's *Inheritors*—you remember the book?' I nodded. 'A horrifying situation when you think of it,' he went on. 'Sitting on the outside watching a new kind of civilisation growing up and knowing it's the end of their old life. It is, believe me, John. The country's on the brink of hoisting itself into the twentieth century.'

'Is that why the Major decided to knock out one of the ape-men?' Dai asked seriously; and when Malcolm turned to him in puzzlement he said, 'The Major man tried to shoot a peasant. He would have killed him if the boss hadn't knocked his little gun up.'

I was embarrassed without understanding why, and all I could do was shrug.

'I hardly think he meant to shoot a peasant.' Malcolm smiled. 'He's a very responsible young man. I think you'll like him, John. He probably wanted to fire a shot to show that you weren't easy game.'

'It's possible.' It was possible. I don't like making my mind up too fast about other people's intentions. 'I would like to go out and see the roadworks today if I can.'

Malcolm reached into his pocket and handed me a ring with two keys on it.

'The four-wheel drive, to your specification. It's parked

at the front of the hotel.' He chuckled. 'You'll find most things well organised. Do you want a guide?' But looking at my face he chuckled again and said, 'I know, you can read maps. I ought to know how competent you are by this time, John. Oh. There's a man you'll meet up there later. Lott. He'll be available for any help you need. Recruiting. Admin and so on.'

'I don't usually need much help,' I said.

'Of course. But he knows the local situation. Look in later if you can. The pink house at the south end of town just beyond the big fountain. Myra's anxious to meet you.'

'I don't like to impose,' I said, and he smiled and shook his head.

'We want to see a lot of you. Both of you, of course. Can I leave you now? If you can't manage this evening we'll get together tomorrow.'

We all stood up again and shook hands, and Malcolm left. Dai sat down and poured himself another drink. He drank a lot, and I waited for him to say something. He didn't say anything. I went into my room and got the charts out and we looked at them for a while.

'Now?' Dai asked me, and I said, 'Why not?' We took jackets and sunglasses and went out to the front. There was a diesel half-tonner parked at the entrance, nicely cleaned, and I drove. It wasn't a bad-looking town. Most of it was old, the Victorian stuff fitted in among the older buildings of stucco or rough stone. The main street north-and-south was quite wide, either by long-ago accident or to accommodate parades in bygone days when Tatra had imperial ambitions. Three or four modern stores in concrete, but not too obtrusive, and one six-storey block of flats visible towards the sea above the low tiled roofs. The biggest pile was the government palace, colonial-Palladian with two or three acres of lawn in front of it and two fountains and a lot of shallow marble steps and balustrades.

'It's as busy as Tiger Bay,' Dai said. 'On a wet Sunday morning.'

'Sensible people are sleeping off lunch,' I suggested. On a long high wall bordering a park or an estate somebody had used an aerosol paint spray to print BOKA LIVES.

'That must be nice for him,' Dai said.

'Probably some kind of coffee.'

The road was well made and wide enough for about four miles, as the charts had promised. Four miles represented the point where the previous government had run out of credit. North from there it was plain dirt, narrow and washed and ground into humps and pot-holes. We were into the foothills and mountains again, but it wasn't as dreary as I had expected. The broad plain was probably glacial, and among the hollows and hillocks stretching out and trembling in the sun there were plenty of stretches of green and yellow and some kind of pinkish vegetation, a lot of it divided by straight lines and obviously cultivated; and as well as scattered houses glaring white there were clusters big enough to be called villages. They were all at some distance from the road, which clearly had no connection with the old natural routes.

Short of a donkey, the half-tonner was about the only feasible transport over the unmade section, and I drove slowly and studied it, and Dai took out the charts and did the same.

'Not at all bad,' he admitted grudgingly. 'Who did it?'

'I don't know.' I eased the front wheels out of a rut. 'A German outfit. They lost their shirts when the old government went bust.'

'Maybe we should ask for our pay in advance, boss,' he muttered. 'It's going to take one heck of a lot of money, innit?'

'You'll get paid.' I laughed at him. 'If Malcolm's in it, it's solid.'

'Yes, he knows his way about, your old Malcolm,' Dai said. This pleased me, but he added, 'Married to a countess too, I would describe your old Malcolm as a trustworthy citizen, boy.'

It always had to be boss or boy.

'What about it?' I sneered at him. 'Don't tell me you're an upside-down Welsh snob.'

'No, no, nothin' of the kind, I applaud the entire thing, honest, I wouldn't mind that myself and to hell with my mam. Do you have to bow before you jump into bed with a countess? I'm only askin', it's a novel speculation, see?'

'No,' I said, 'but you have to wear an ermine nightshirt.' It was no use trying to be superior with Dai. Knowing Malcolm, I was pretty sure that if he had married a countess it was because he happened to like that particular woman. But I couldn't be solemn about it. A cloud of dust appeared on the road far ahead, and I started to look for a slightly wider stretch where two vehicles could pass. I found one when the cloud had approached to within two hundred yards, drew over to the side, and waited.

The cloud identified itself as another half-tonner, but instead of coming alongside and inching past, it squealed to a stop where the road narrowed again. I waited for a few seconds, and then waved it on. It didn't move. A tall thin figure vaulted out of the driving seat and walked towards us; an army officer, with one hand resting on his pistol holster.

'I'll tell him you didn't see the red light,' Dai said, and I said, 'Could you try to keep your mouth shut? Please?'

Dai pouted and sank down in his seat. The officer stopped a yard away and bored into me with his steely eyes, and two of his fingers fumbled invisibly with the holster flap.

'This truck is government property,' he said.

'Yes,' I said.

'Who are you?' he said.

'Who are you?' I said.

'Who I am is not your affair. Where are your papers?'

'If you let me know who you are I'll talk about my papers. I can't be too careful,' I said.

'I am Captain Daren.' He was half reluctant and half eager to supply the name. He was tall and about twenty-eight and palpably an adolescent pup trying to impersonate an Alsatian.

'The son of the President?'

'I am Captain Daren.'

'Nice to meet you,' I said. 'I am John Carlyle. I'm the road engineer for Tatra Mines.'

He turned this over unwillingly.

'Can you prove that?' he demanded.

'No.' I shook my head in apology, concerned at giving him so much trouble. 'I've got no papers on me except the road charts.'

'That isn't satisfactory. Who are you?' he snapped at Dai. Dai shrugged and touched his lips.

'He is Mr David Owen,' I said, and the officer barked at me:

'I was speaking to him.'

'Tell the gentleman who you are, David,' I said, and Dai said:

'I am Mr David Owen, sir.'

'Your papers.'

Silently Dai handed him the charts. Daren's natural superiority rose above his embarrassment and he smiled thinly and said, 'You will return with me to Victoria.' He handed the charts back to Dai, who took them with his right hand and affected to salute with his left, changed his mind, waved his hands about and got a finger stuck in one ear.

'Oh dear,' I said, 'I'm terribly sorry, Captain, this must be very inconvenient, but unfortunately I'm on urgent government business and I can't manage it at the moment. Maybe I could drop in later?'

As far as I could tell, apart from my first brusque retort, I had worked hard to be nice to the boy and let him save his face. But he wasn't enjoying me at all. He stood slapping his holster with his open palm, a gesture designed to paralyse the evildoer with terror, and while I looked regretful and helpful, he finally said:

'I shall have to check on your credentials. I hope for your sake they are genuine.'

Dismissing us with a glare, he swung smartly and strode back to his vehicle. I clapped my hand over Dai's mouth in case he started to whistle in rhythm. The Captain started up his truck, let out the clutch and shrieked past us in a sandstorm, looking neither to the left nor to the right.

'I'll slay you,' I told Dai.

'Me? Nothin', I said, I said nothin' at all, boy, it was you that was doin' the big comedy performance.'

'I was polite and restrained.' I meant it. Dai roared with laughter.

'You are a hell of an actor, boy, the derision was spilling out of you, if I was your little soldier I would have shot you and then stamped on you.'

I started the truck and drove forward, deeply worried. If I was in Tatra to build a road—or anywhere to do anything—my idea always was to get along with people whether I liked them or not. I regarded myself as a placid person who could swallow dislike or anger because both emotions were a waste of time. But, of course, with Dai you could never tell. He was probably projecting his own derision on to me.

'There's a lot of complications in Tatra they didn't tell you about, boss. You should be a worried man.'

'What's life without a few complications?' I concentrated on driving, but I must still have been thinking about the young captain, because a few minutes later I said, 'You're right, Dai, Captain Daren doesn't like us much. Screw him.'

'Somebody has. Funny thing you should say that, boy, he had the look of a man who has just put in some extra-mural study.'

'What makes you think that?'

'I never think about anything else, do I? I know the signs, boy, I served my apprenticeship in knowing the signs.'

'He should have been happy and lovable in that case.'

'You can never tell, boy, maybe he didn't hit the old jackpot an' he's sore about his old manhood.'

'You're mad,' I told him. 'Nobody lives this far north except peasants and fishermen. These military Tats have a caste system harder than the Indians.'

'Indeed indeed, the polo-playing sewers, and what is a caste system for if it isn't to give the top boys a free supply of working-class shack-ups, boy!'

'Politics politics,' I said. 'Eight months should do this job if the machines get here in time.'

'Listen to me talkin', would you, I'm only thinkin' of a good ration of peasant myself, my mam would beat me to death. Yes, these Germans know somethin' about road-buildin'.'

It was going to take a lot of bottoming to turn the dirt track into a two-lane road, but I was almost unconsciously noting the useful bits of mountain as I drove and I knew that Dai was doing the same thing, roughly calculating blasting points and quantities and truck runs. We worked so easily together that we could agree at this stage without even speaking our thoughts. I found myself nodding speculatively at a big outcrop of gneiss above the track, and noticed him nodding at the same thing at the same time, and we both laughed. Building roads is a good job. You see something for your money and you don't do anybody any particular harm.

But I decided Dai was right about the complications. All the jobs we had done together before were in Britain, and the difficulties were routine, rain or frost or the occasional outbreak of red tape or bloodymindedness. I didn't want to know anything about the politics of Tatra, I didn't want them to get in the way of the job, and if the island had a military government all I wanted from it was to be left alone. At least, I thought, a military government would believe in getting things done; better than a crowd of little politicians and bureaucrats with private squabbles and their hands in the till.

We got to within a mile of the mine site, the dirt track faded away and I got the truck turned and started back. The afternoon was getting late, and I remembered that in this Mediterranean latitude the sun would go crashing down without any English twilight nonsense.

When we were almost back at the metalled road I saw a crowd of men or boys straggling about the dirt track. I didn't bother hooting because the noise of the engine was audible for miles; but as we drew close to them, they stayed where they were. Some were squatting by the roadside, some were sitting on the track itself. One youth was strumming a kind of triangular ukelele, with his head bent towards the strings to hear what he was playing. There were about a dozen of them. I stopped and went into neutral. They turned and looked at us with the faintest of interest. The one with the ukelele waved languidly and said something I couldn't hear above the noise of the motor. I switched it off, and Dai's hand went out to stop me switching it off, but I shrugged and said, 'We can't drive over them.'

A wispy-bearded boy ambled up to the truck and said, 'Go with love.'

'We can't go anywhere, boy,' Dai told him, 'without using your family as tarmacadam.'

'You are English,' the boy said triumphantly.

'Welsh, boy, Welsh, get it right.'

One of the other youths was leaning on the other side of the truck, either dazed or slightly drunk, and he said, 'I know Welsh—you are an oppressed minority group.'

'One Welshman is a majority anywhere,' Dai said amiably. 'We are not so easy oppressed, boy.'

'Go with love,' said the second boy.

'Is it a love-in?' I asked. I wasn't at all sure of the crowd, but they seemed harmless and the wisest thing was to be friendly in any case, since our truck didn't have a carbine under the dashboard like the Major's car. The bearded boy shook his head sadly.

'No girls,' he complained.

'A booze-in, then,' Dai suggested.

'We're not drunk,' the bearded boy giggled. 'We're liberated.'

'I know, boy,' Dai said in sympathy. 'It gets me the same way.'

A fat boy smiling owlishly right in front of the truck, cried, 'Boka lives!'

'True, true,' several of them chanted.

'Boka lives!'

'True, true!'

'That is clever of him,' Dai said, but already the boy was bashing at the ukelele and they started up a discordant chorus.

'The tree grows up from the sand
Because a tree must grow
The sand lies still in the sun
It has nowhere to go

21

And Boka lives
Boka lives
Sing oh brothers sing
Boka lives . . .'

Somebody started a second verse, but half of them repeated the first—it's always the same with these chorus
songs, once any group is more than three people the pro-
portion who know all the words drops by a geometric
progression. So the rest of the song was a rabble and the
first chorus was the only one I could remember.

They were all wearing jeans and sandals, some of them
had scruffy tee-shirts and others faded flowery shirts
hanging outside their trousers. A couple had gussets sewn
into the bottoms of their jeans to convert them to bell-
bottoms. The boy with the ukelele had several strings of
beads, and three of the other boys wore patterned bands
round their foreheads. They looked like a poverty-stricken
rustic attempt to live up to San Francisco or the swinging
London scene which they had dimly observed in out-of-
date magazines.

'Do you want a lift?' I yelled above the din.

'We own nothing, we need nothing,' the fat boy said
slurrily, but some of the others immediately started to
climb aboard. They all got in, or on, and Dai, after trying
in vain to persuade the fat boy not to lie across in front of
the windscreen, got out and hauled him off and forced him
up among the heap of bodies in the back. It was one way
of getting the truck moving again. I started up, and they
started a strangled repetition of their song when we hit the
tarmac and speeded up.

'It feels like Liverpool,' Dai yelled at me.

The sun was dropping out of sight, and we could see
the lights of Victoria ahead. One of the boys leaned out of
the scrum and started to shout in my ear. The others were

still singing. I slowed down in an effort to hear him, and he stuck an upraised thumb in front of my eyes to signal his appreciation so that I had to slam on the brakes to avoid running off the road. The boys tumbled off and lurched about on the road, and the musician shouted, 'Go with love!' They all joined in this chorus too. Dai and I waved, and I started up and went into town.

I met Dai in the bar of the Louis before dinner. I had had the half-hearted idea of having a sandwich and spending the evening in private, annotating the roadworks charts and starting on a draft of a schedule, but Dai protested that where there was a bar there was a bird and that man didn't live by charts alone; and there was nothing very useful I could do theoretically till we got properly to work in the field. So I met Dai in the bar of the Louis.

There were birds, but all with male birds, and few of them looked very exciting in any case. The bar was converted to American-style with low lighting and dense carpeting, but the atmosphere was still deeply familiar and respectable and nearly everybody was sitting in groups at tables while we put our elbows on the long bar. The barman had a mauve linen jacket with the nameplate George stuck to the breast pocket.

'That kind of thing nearly got me thrown out of a pub in Birmingham,' I told Dai. 'There was a busty waitress with Gladys printed on one side of her overall, and I asked her what the other one was called.'

'You quiet polite people are always dangerous company, boss,' he said. 'Two large vodkas, George, and two blondes.'

'The vodkas I can give you.' George smiled sadly. 'This is a very respectable country.'

'Too respectable?' Dai asked him. Certainly it was hard to tell whether George was boasting or complaining.

He said quickly, 'I didn't say that, sir.'

'But I can think what I like,' said Dai.

'*You* can, sir. I have no opinions, I'm a barman.'

Dai wasn't worried. In any country, however respectable, there are always birds for somebody like Dai who is prepared to find them. And for me, if it comes to that, although I didn't go on about them all the time as he did. Outside, from some distance away, came the tuneless chorus of Boka Lives.

'Our celestial choir again,' Dai said, and I asked the Barman, 'Who is Boka?'

His face was blank.

'It's a song, sir, kids sing anything these days.'

A police whistle sounded. Scattered shouts could be heard above the singing.

'A parade,' Dai said. 'Let's have a look, boss.'

'It's best to pay no attention, sir,' George said. In fact, I hadn't been going to pay any attention, but I don't like being told. Dai was already strolling towards the big plate-glass front door of the bar, and I took my drink and followed him out to the hotel forecourt. The other customers at the tables either looked up and looked away, or didn't look up at all.

Three boys, who might in the dim light have been three of our hitch-hikers, were pelting along the main street pursued by a policeman or a soldier—there didn't seem to be much difference. Across the street from us they suddenly spread out, and as the policeman turned indecisively after one of them, another darted behind him and knocked his hat off and gave a little chuckle of triumph. It was a gay student lark, like Boat Race night in Piccadilly.

Another policeman pounded along waving a stick and smashed it down at the boy's head. The kid crumpled in the gutter and the second policeman clouted him another glancing blow on the shoulder as he fell. The first policeman picked up his hat, turned and swung the boot at the boy. Dai shot forward and I grabbed for his arm. I was sick, but there was nothing we could do that would help. Dai was too quick for me. He did a hurdling jump, landed on one foot on the tailboard of the half-tonner and his second jump landed him in the front seat. The horn of the truck roared and its headlights went on simultaneously.

With the truck facing the roadway slightly askew, the lights didn't get the boy dead centre, but they lit him up all right, and the two policemen, and the horn jerked them round to be blinded. The first one, with his hand in front of his face, jumped out of the beam and galloped towards us. The second was slower, and while he was blinking, the boy in the gutter scrambled to hands and knees and scuttled into the darkness like a cat.

Trouble trouble trouble. The policeman on the run was just coming back into the beam as he ran through the centre opening in the low wall of the forecourt, and I jumped down beside the truck without an idea in my head. The headlamps went off. Relatively unblinded because I had been standing behind them, I saw the policeman falter in his stride as the darkness struck him. I still had my glass, hardly spilled.

'What's going on, officer?' I laid it on thick, both the accent and the asperity, but it didn't stop him. He jumped towards the sound of my voice with the stick working. I nipped aside and let him trip on to the stone verandah; and before he could think of anything else I grabbed him one-handed by the collar and yanked him to his feet and barked, 'Stand to attention!'

He swayed about and grunted, but the voice got through to something this time. He swithered between standing to attention and splitting my skull open, and I took a horrible chance and turned and snapped at his mate, 'You! Come here!'

The second policeman lumbered into the forecourt, and while they were both still indecisive, I furtively stepped back on the verandah, giving myself about a foot advantage in height.

The second one was also frothing adrenalin, and he hadn't been winded by falling on his face. He snarled, 'Obstructing the police! You . . .'

I cut through this with another bark.

'Attention when you speak to me! You're a disgrace! What is your duty?'

'It's a riot!' He was still hoping to murder me, or anybody convenient. 'Who switched the lights on?'

'My chauffeur,' I said, and before this insanity could go any further I added, 'A riot, eh? Good men! Carry on! Jeeves! The door,' I gestured towards the bar door with my head, and Dai was there in one leap.

'Yes, sir!' He pushed the door ajar, and I nodded to the two gorillas and strode through. Dai was right on my heels. I stopped striding the second I was through, and we lapsed into an ambling stroll back to Charles. Charles was busy rubbing a glass out of existence.

'A lot of people shouting out there,' I said. 'I couldn't see anything.'

'Drunk, I suppose,' said Dai.

'It sometimes happens, sir.' Charles was won round again.

'Double up on the vodkas,' I said.

'With pleasure, sir.'

When Charles was safely at the other end of the bar, Dai looked into his glass and murmured, 'I don't know that I exactly like the Jeeves idea—my mam always said he was a traitor to the proletariat even if he was a good old scream.'

'Did you want me to use your own name?' I murmured into my glass. 'I had to get both of us in here fast.'

'Ah, I'm not complaining, boss, we did all right. One Welshman can still outnumber any twenty foreigners even when he's only got an Englishman to help him out. But my own idea would have been more artistic.'

'What was it?'

'To kick the coppers' faces in. Their faces are too convex, you have to admit that.'

I tried to release a great sigh without deafening everybody in the bar.

'We'll just stay away from any kind of trouble,' I told Dai, and he said:

'I hope we're not still in it, boy?'

'Why?'

'The cops are still out there, and there's one of the kids lyin' shiverin' under the half-tonner.'

'Oh, yes. He can damn well shiver.'

3

I FOUND that we couldn't let him shiver without at least knowing whether he was going to get clear. We finished our drinks and went very casually back to my suite, and I cursed Dai for being a meddling maniac.

'We'll never build roads here if we're doing ten years in jail,' I said. 'I don't know anything about their politics...'

'They stink.'

'... maybe they stink, but we're foreigners and we're here to work and be good. The Tats speak English, but they're not English and they're not Welsh either...'

'By the living God, boy, they're not Welsh!'

'... and they've got their own way of running things. From now on it's blinkers and ear-muffs, get it?'

'Right, boss.'

'We've probably done enough to get ten years already,' I said, and I wasn't joking. 'Thank God Malcolm's in big with the Cabinet and the President.'

'Right, boss.'

'If you say right boss again I'll trample you.'

'Right, boss.'

'Right.'

'And what about the kid under the truck?'

'Oh hell.'

'My very words, boss.'

I was tired of the whole affair. I slumped in a chair and said, 'I suppose we'll have to go for a ride somewhere.'

'But not naked into the world, boy.' He went through the connecting door to his suite, and, frankly, I took a swig from the gin bottle, for the want of anything better to do. Dai came back with his heavy old bag, the job bag, and opened it on my table, and started to lay out tools on the table in a neat row. He's good with tools. Apart from being a great foreman he's one of the best untrained mechanics anywhere and he likes the feel and the shape of implements. Finally he picked out a wrecking bar, about eighteen inches long, hooked nastily at one end; and a pipe-wrench about the same size; and one of the shifting spanners he used on the big nuts on the earthmovers.

'I don't intend to misuse good tools,' he apologised, 'but the next man I meet with a club will expect a fair fight at least. Not that I would be quixotic. Here.' He flipped a cap at me, and I caught it and threw it on the floor.

'We're not going to meet any more men with clubs,' I told him fiercely. 'Tonight was an unlucky accident. Any more of this nonsense and you're going back to your bloody mountains and coal-tips.'

'You can't run a truck without a bit of a repair kit,' he said in bland innocence. 'And you want a cap in this climate for the sunstroke.'

The caps were Dai's own invention. When we worked on a bridge job for Chorley-Copland he took a bitter dislike to the standard fibreglass safety helmets they issued, because he complained that they made him look like an upturned chamber-pot with feet. They were certainly bulky and he was small. So he made a plaster mould and laid up half a dozen fibreglass helmets derived from ski caps. He claimed they attracted a completely different type of bird.

'We have to set an example to the peasant workers,' he said reasonably. 'Safety first and safety all the time, boy. Not only that,' he added, 'but it gives the poor storm-troopers a nice chance to play tunes with their clubs while

29

you're peacefully kicking in their old virility symbols, eh, boy?'

It was possible that he was wise. Anyway, if people heaved boulders down cliffs a safety helmet was mandatory. We put on one each and carried the others out to the truck with the tools, avoiding the bar.

The police, or army or whatever, were decidedly still on the job. There was a distinctly unpleasant feeling about the streets, sporadic shouts coming from various directions, the odd distant whistle, and the sound of heavy knocking, as of somebody breaking in to kill or begging in to be saved. We put the weapons under the dashboard and heaved the spare caps in the rear seat and Dai said softly, 'Are you still there, boy?'

There was no answer. He got on hands and knees and looked under the truck and said, 'It's only the minstrel boy, boy, get into the truck quick.'

The ukelele boy rolled out into the open and slithered aboard the truck. There was no place in it to hide anybody. After a glance at him I took Dai's jacket from him and gave it to the boy, and put a cap on his head.

'Good gear,' he said happily. He wasn't nearly as nervous as I was. I was nervous. 'So where's the action?'

'The action's here,' I said brusquely, 'that's why we're leaving.'

'Sure, sure. Being kicked to death is a drag, let's find another scene.'

'What's on tonight?' Dai asked him. I sat and fiddled with the truck key to waste time while two policemen walked purposefully past the hotel.

'Ah, it's only the bang-squad's menstrual boot-fest,' the kid said. 'Man, they dig that lunar influence.'

'What were you doing to annoy them?' I demanded. I never enjoyed the conformity of hip talk, and it was even more of an irritant from this bucolic infant.

'Man, they're self-generating—when their ovaries tell them to go, they go. It's the law,' he added a little more comprehensibly. 'More than ten bodies together is a political demonstration. Are you subversives?'

'I'm an engineer,' I said.

'You're a gasser, man,' he corrected me. 'A real gasser, you make dialogue like a dream man, you have a role.'

'No thanks.' I realised this was slightly funny while I was saying it, and I added, 'I've already eaten.' The kid liked the small joke. I edged the truck out into the street and turned south, because I wanted to see Malcolm again and get some reassurance and because any direction was good enough for the kid, I imagined. The main street ran straight and true for miles, and quite a long way off I was pretty sure I could see the lights, both still and moving, of what was probably a road block. I was about to turn right into a side street when down the side street I saw five or six policemen dragging people out of a café and flailing about with their sticks. I straightened the wheels up and went slowly on.

'Maybe he's right about the menstrual fest,' I said to Dai. 'It would be funny if all the women in Tatra had synchronised periods and their husbands went berserk with frustration the same night.'

'No go, man,' the kid chipped in, 'except they have periods every week. Man, what a pace to live at.'

It was absolutely ridiculous to be worried about a road block. I was a guest, and a damned important guest, of the damned country, and I was more important to the Government than fifty riot troopers. And the kid in the back was simply a kid, not doing anything illegal but being given a ride in a truck. All I needed to do was to tell any policeman I met that I was on my way to Sir Malcolm's and he would jump aside and salute.

'We'll talk our way through that block,' I said to Dai.

'Sure, boss.' He had entire confidence in me.

But a second or so later, away ahead beyond the block, I saw headlights rushing in our direction, and the approaching vehicle roared straight through the block and kept coming at us. I tucked well into my own side and trundled, and it howled past for a hundred yards and then squealed round the corner I had nearly turned. It was the same truck, the same colour, as I was driving. Without waiting to think twice, I snapped on my own headlights and rammed the throttle down. A diesel takes a while to wind up, and it probably wouldn't top sixty-five, but sixty-five is fast enough.

'What are you going to do, boy?' Dai yelled. 'Run over them?'

'They'll think we're the other truck on the way back,' I yelled. However illogical, I felt safer belting along at sixty than stopping to chat to anybody on the menstrual boot-fest night. 'He's got me saying it,' I muttered while the road block rushed up at us through the white tunnel of the lamps. In fact, it was fairly casual, half a dozen lanterns sitting on the roadside and half a dozen apathetic cops lounging beside them with electric torches, probably bored for want of a few kidneys to kick. They hardly glanced as we went through them, and after a drenching with the headlamps they would hardly have seen us anyway.

I travelled another two miles till the road curved away and the habitations thinned out. Then I stopped and switched off the lights, and the kid said, 'Ping ping ping, man, you're telekinetic. Is the gear for keeps?' He jumped out of the truck, and Dai took him by the arm and said, 'Not on your life, boy. I'm property-conscious.'

'So we all have our troubles.'

The kid peeled off the jacket and took off the cap and handed them over, and I said, 'Are you sure you didn't start a riot?'

'Man, a riot here is when you stand still and breathe in public.'

'Do you ever beat the cops?' Dai asked him, and the kid looked contemptuous and said:

'You kill an animal, you *are* an animal. Boka he say.'

'Who the hell is Boka?' I demanded.

'Boka?' The kid seemed surprised at the question. 'Man, Boka's a man. Boka lives.'

'Is that all he does?' I asked. 'Live?'

'Man, who lives? You live, maybe? You breathe, you sweat, you eat. Me, I live in twitches when I get it. Boka *lives*. True true.'

'You're a nut,' I said.

'A nut feels it too, maybe. If chestnuts could scream, vegetarians would die. Boka he say.'

'Some people would sicken you,' Dai said happily, and the kid said, 'Go with love,' and vanished across a field.

I made a U-turn and started back with dipped lights. The big fountain was obvious enough, though I hadn't noticed it consciously on the way out. So was the pink house, with a high pink wall and wrought-iron gates, closed. I stopped and got out and pulled an old-fashioned bell on the wall. Immediately a policeman padded along the pavement and shone a torch in my face.

'Your papers,' he snarled.

'They're at my hotel, sorry.' They weren't. My passport was in my pocket. But the principle was wrong. And he couldn't have taken me for a rioting teenager. I was too old and too big.

'Your name.'

'John Carlyle,' I said, and I kept it friendly because I was getting tired of policemen and I knew that could be dangerous. 'I'm calling on Sir Malcolm.'

'John!' It was Malcolm himself. He was swinging half of the gate open. The torch swung on to his face, and he smiled into it and said, 'That's rather bright, Sergeant. Can I help you?'

'Sorry, Sir Malcolm.' The cop sprang to attention and put the torch out.

'That's all right, Sergeant,' Malcolm said kindly. 'Is your friend with you, John?' Dai vaulted out of the truck and stood beside me. 'Good night, Sergeant,' Malcolm said. 'Oh you'd better take a good look at Mr Carlyle and Mr Owen, they're very important people in Tatra.'

'Yes, sir.' The sergeant peered at us without using the torch. We went through the gate, and Malcolm put us one on either side of him and put his hands on our shoulders as we walked up the drive.

'I'm glad you came,' he said. 'We're having a nice dull domestic evening. They're here, Myra.'

A tallish woman was silhouetted against the light of the open door. She stepped back into the hall as we reached her. She looked a few years older than myself, about thirty-five or thirty-six, thin but healthy looking. Long light brown hair, caught in a clasp at the back and hanging down —not a ponytail or anything stylish, merely caught out of the way and hanging. Her teeth and her chin were too long. It's true, some English aristocrats have horsy faces to live up to their caricatures.

'Howdydo. Mr Carlyle. Mr Owen.'

I shook her hand and said howdydo. Her grip was firm but she was trembling slightly, maybe from coming out of a warm room.

'Hello, Mrs Wreford,' Dai said. 'Do I call you Mrs Wreford or Lady Myra or what? I've never had the problm see, and my mam never thought to tell me.'

Malcolm laughed uproariously, and Myra blushed and said, 'Malcolm hopes—I hope you'll call me Myra. I believe your name is Dai.'

'That's right. At home they call me Dai the death,'

he said. 'Can I go to the bog? I'm full up to here with vodka'.

'There's one here.' Malcolm opened the door of a cloak-room leading off the hall.

I suspected that he wasn't sure whether Dai was drunk or not, and I said, 'It's all right, he talks like that all the time.'

In fact, I think he had picked up this particular social gambit from myself. When in doubt, infantile honesty is the game. I couldn't tell how it had gone down with Malcolm's wife. She was a rather twitchy lady, I decided. We went into a long low-ceilinged lounge and Dai followed us and when she went to the sideboard to get drinks he went with her to help.

'You go in a lot for policemen here,' I said to Malcolm, and he smiled and said:

'They are a bit obvious—it's a hangover from the change of government when things looked as if they might be unsettled. It's a serious danger of military regimes—they're always liable to be more interested in order than in law.'

'I saw two of them trying to kick a boy stupid for no particular reason.'

'You didn't interfere,' he said quickly, and I shook my head, and from the sideboard Dai, overhearing, looked across at me and got the message.

'The kid got away,' I told Malcolm. Dai came over with a tray and Malcolm's wife gave me a vodka and Malcolm an orange juice, and then Dai purposefully took the tray to the sofa and sat her down and sat beside her. A bird, even a married rather horsy-faced bird (I'm not being cruel, she wasn't unattractive), was always preferable in Dai's view to a man of any kind.

'That's one of the reasons why I decided to leave the Agricultural Development Agency for a couple of years and take on this job,' Malcolm told me. 'There's no reason why a military government shouldn't be a good government but if it can have a moderating influence, so much the better. The President's a big man. A big man. You'll meet him, of course.'

'Have you not eaten at all?' I heard Myra asking Dai, and he said:

'You know 'ow it is, you get talkin'—I wouldn't mind a nice old corned-beef sandwich.' The working-class Welsh lilt was nearly a caricature. 'Will I come to the kitchen an' 'elp you then, or do you 'ave thousands of underpaid slaveys makin' food night an' day?'

Malcolm glanced at them and then turned back to me as Myra got up and went to the door with Dai trotting beside her.

'It's a far cry from the old radical studies group, isn't it?' he said. 'Advising an upper-class military junta.'

'So is road-building.' I didn't think there was anything wrong with Malcolm's advising a military junta. It would be good advice.

'You've done very well,' he said. 'I've heard about your progress from time to time, Lord, it's too long since we saw each other, John. Time, there's never enough time. The Hooper Commission and then the Export Board and then the Agency. Ah, the years slip away. No, I was talking about the government. The island needs firm management, there's no doubt about that. The old crowd—I have no personal knowledge, of course, but they were obviously a fumbling lot. The economy's pretty disastrous still. But I imagine—I'm sure—that when the country's on its feet the thing will evolve into something more representative.'

'Government of the people by the people and for the people.'

Malcolm smiled reminiscently.

'Democracy is a pretty stubborn growth even if it flops from time to time. Don't worry, John, I haven't changed my principles. Remember *Experiments in Prosperity?*'

'How can I forget it?' I held up my wrist with the gold watch he had given me when the book was published. It had been a quite unexpected thank you for the few bits of research I had helped him with.

'My my. It's a long time ago, isn't it? I suppose in a way I had to end up here. It isn't a grass-roots democracy experiment, but it's fascinating. Tatra is a kind of test-bench, I couldn't resist it, of course—the chance to see how some of our old notions could work in real life.'

'Like playing with toy trains.' I smiled, and he laughed.

'I could never resist *trying* things,' he said.

'How much power... freedom, I mean... have you got?'

'*Carte blanche.*' He spread his hands. 'The old general knew when he took over that he had no experience of industry or irrigation or any of that boring civilian stuff. The don't teach it at Sandhurst. Hence me. I hope it's a good thing. But if he hadn't pushed the old government aside, I suspect the Communists would have moved in.'

'Are there many Communists?'

'Who knows? They'd be well underground now, in any case. But we know that it doesn't take many. You look fine and fit, John—honestly, it's good to see you.'

'The road shouldn't be too difficult,' I said. 'The German company did a good job before they chucked it. Is it Communists the riot police are after?'

'Go on then, love, play somethin',' I heard Dai say, through a mouthful of sandwich. 'I'm daft about the old piano, honest.' Myra didn't seem eager to play the piano. Malcolm was looking worried and concerned.

'Paris, Germany, Alabama,' he said. 'The student thing, the teenager thing—it's a universal manifestation, isn't it? The dangerous thing is that it provokes a violent backlash, of course. I don't like it, I don't like it at all, it's one of the things I'm trying to moderate. But . . .' He smiled. 'I'm afraid I sometimes come round to the cynical old dictum

37

of not interfering unless you know you can achieve something. It's not a very noble principle, is it?'

'I don't know. I wouldn't try to catch an escaped lion. Who is Boka, Malcolm?'

Myra started to play the piano. Debussy. Dai was beside her, to turn the pages of the music. Malcolm smiled over towards them and said, 'There are some things to be said for a ladylike education.'

'I never congratulated you on your marriage.'

'Thank you, John.'

Touched, he reached over and touched my arm. 'Lord knows I left it late enough. But it's deeply rewarding. Deeply rewarding.' He chuckled. 'It's a laugh, when you think of the old days. How will I feel if I become the father of a viscount? What a joke!'

'Bloody marvellous,' I said.

Myra came to the end of the faun's afternoon and looked round to see what we were laughing at, but Malcolm waved a hand and said, 'Just a private old joke, Myra.' She smiled, uncertainly and started to play 'Where'er You Walk'. Dai came in with the voice right on the button. I was a bit puzzled about Dai. He liked birds young, and he usually liked them on the roly-poly side. But, of course, he liked birds. And he did like music. A bloody caricature stage-Welshman, with the full *hwyl* or whatever they call it. No, that wasn't fair, the voice had dropped the nonsense and was coming out silver pure and clean, and Myra was glancing up at him in surprise and smiling nervously. There was nothing Malcolm and I could do but listen. Tenors are sexy sods, Dai had often told me. Malcolm closed his eyes to concentrate on the sound. I kept mine open to enjoy the long lines of the room and the pale colours at the same time.

Malcolm applauded.

'Beautiful. Thank you, Dai.'

'It *was* beautiful,' Myra said.

'It is all an old fake, indeed to goodness,' Dai said cheerfully. 'John is a ventriloquist. Now give Beethoven a good old bash, love.'

As she struck a tentative chord, I said to Malcolm, 'Who is Boka?'

'Oh yes. Oh dear. Honestly, I'm beginning to wonder if it's anybody.'

'I thought at first it was an advertisement for coffee,' I told him, and he laughed, not very happily.

'It's the same thing again. Castro, Che Guevara, Tariq Ali—sometimes I wonder if they're real people or simply symbols invented by the young. I imagine it's a passing trend like the Beatles.'

'The Beatles are hanging on pretty long,' I suggested, and he nodded sadly.

'I don't really know much about the man, or the thing, or whatever it is, John, but that's the kind of thing it is as I analyse it. I don't suppose there's much harm in it, on the surface. But these . . . these upsurges, ground swells, fads, call them what you like . . . they're always in danger of manipulation.'

'By the Communists?'

'You really go at it like a terrier, don't you, John.' He shook his head in a kind of affectionate paternal admiration. I was surprised.

'Do I? I was just curious. We met some kids today. Go with love, they said. It didn't sound very dangerous. Daft, maybe.'

'Go with love, yes, go with love.' Malcolm sounded faintly weary. 'There is the object, and there is the image, and the image drains the meaning from the object, and the word becomes the thing, and then the thing is a different thing under the same word. Sorry to sound so obstruse, but the evolution of words away from meanings is just about the most baffling aspect of sociology to me. To simplify by analogy'—we glanced at each other comfortably— 'always remembering that analogy is not necessarily in itself a method of proof, but rather of illumination, eh ?' We were back in the radical studies group, enjoying one of Malcolm's tutorials. 'The equality of man means the equality of man . . . in so far as it can mean anything. Accepted: that Capitalism promotes the inequality of man. Proposed: that Communism should be established to promote the equality of man. Communism is established. The equality of man is achieved. But to make men equal, some men must govern. Some men must be killed. Some men must be imprisoned. Hey presto, the inequality of man, now entitled the equality of man.'

'Or the doctrine of Christian fellowship,' I added dutifully, 'preached by the Inquisition by incineration.'

'The point is made and taken. I don't know, John. I have an instinctive sympathy with the young. But they're the champions at the game of swallowing a slogan for the mere sound of it. I don't know whether they love everybody or whether they'll use the word love as a truncheon. There is somebody called Boka. Probably a harmless enough youngster with some of that half-baked mysticism everybody is importing from India. He roams about up in the north.'

'Are the police after him ?' I asked.

'Not particularly, no. They would crack down on him if they caught him preaching to a crowd—there's a temporary ban on political gatherings. But no, not particularly. The administration is pretty loose up there, of course, with such a scattered population. That's one of the things the new road will help. That, and the development of the mines.'

I didn't know that this was an added incentive to building the new road, but it was none of my business. I wasn't too much concerned about Boka or anything else in Tatra, my questions were simply for information because I can't stand not knowing things. Sitting in the low graceful lounge with Myra now playing one of the sweet-sad Chopin nocturnes, I found it hard to believe that I had nearly got into a fight with two police thugs an hour earlier. I enjoyed the music, and I would build the road and keep life as simple as it could be kept in this dangerous little island.

Later a maid brought in coffee and soft sweet chocolate cake and we guzzled it and took it as the signal to leave. Myra seemed genuinely sorry.

'I don't often play,' she said to me.

'I try to persuade her often enough,' Malcolm said. He came to the door with an arm across his wife's shoulders. 'Obviously it takes a Welshman, eh, Myra?'

She laughed, a bit shakily, and said, 'You'll come again —they'll come again, won't they, Malcolm?'

'You must,' he said warmly. We all shook hands. Dai had stopped his performance and wasn't talking. He and I got into the half-tonner and drove back to the Louis. The police had vanished from the streets and in fact, considering it was well short of midnight, the town was fairly dead. Dai came into my room to have a last swig from the bottle of gin before bed. He was still silent.

'Enjoy the evening?' I asked him. He nodded doubtfully, and after a pause said:

'Your old Malcolm's a very able man, isn't he?'

'He's . . . Yep, he's yes, very able.'

'He seems a kindhearted sort of a chap.' Dai seemed to have lost interest.

'How did you like Myra?' I asked him.

'She isn't a bad pianist at all.'

'You were very thick with her.' I was ready for bed. I started to peel off my shirt.

'I 'ad to let you get on with the old reminiscences, isn't it?' he said. 'Nobody can say my mam didn't teach me manners.' He was probably tired too. He went into his own suite without saying good night.

4

WE had no more than the routine kind of difficulties at the head office of Tatra Mines next morning. It was quite a flash new building down at the dockyard and in fact under the name TATRA MINES were the names Tatra Dockyard Company, Tatra Import-Export Company, Surveys Inc., Tatra Stone and Gravel, Tatra Utilities and Tatra Holdings.

'Busy little place,' Dai said.

'Tatra Mines is the middle of it all,' I said. 'Don't worry, it's all the Tatra government, or most of it, but this way they do the big industrial development like a business and they get outside capital in to help. The government knows what it wants, but instead of the Civil Service lousing it up they appoint Tatra Mines as the chosen instrument.'

'Chosen instrument? It's a bloody symphony orchestra, boy.'

We were shown into the office of a Mr Tasker, plump and jolly. The office was lush. He made a speech of welcome and we had coffee and cigars and talked about the mighty challenge of transforming an entire nation and the value of good communications and overall planning and foresight. It was quite nice. We finally discussed the machinery and the process of getting material, and he summoned his Mr Lott. Papa Lott, everybody called him. Mr Lott was small and quick and eager to please and he hopped from foot to foot a good deal, from nervous energy and enthusiasm. The machines were all in the dockyard warehouses as they had arrived. He was at our service for any arrangements we needed. We needed, I said, four men who could drive.

'Done as soon as asked, Mr Carlyle,' he said. 'A hundred men if you wish.'

'Just four who can drive in the meantime,' I said.

'And later a hundred, Mr Carlyle—as soon as you want them.'

'Later maybe twenty,' I said. He smiled winningly.

'Our labour is not trained to work at your wonderful speed, Mr Carlyle. Better with fifty.'

'We'll start with twenty, all the same.' I patted him on the shoulder to show that I understood he was doing his best. 'It would help if I knew the local wage rates.'

Lott and Tasker looked at each other and pondered, and Mr Lott said, 'Twenty shillings a day?'

Mr Tasker pursed his lips and thought, he said, 'It is higher than the average—we haven't arrived at the age of affluence, Mr Carlyle.'

'The work is harder and more urgent,' Mr Lott pointed out, and Tasker nodded. So Dai and I would take twice as much money as our twenty workers all together. That also was none of my business. You have to pay enough to attract workers, but you can't upset the rest of society by paying too much.

'More for the drivers?' I asked.

'Twenty-five?' said Mr Lott.

'Thirty,' said Mr Tasker.

'You'll want a specimen of my signature for the payroll cheques,' I said.

'There is no need to worry, Mr Carlyle, I will take care of all that,' Papa Lott assured me.

'I don't mind handling my own payrolls,' I said, and

wrote my name on Mr Tasker's desk pad. 'It's the way I usually work.'

'Certainly, I am only here to help.'

'How do I get materials?'

'Ah.' Mr Tasker liked a question he could answer. 'There is no difficulty, everything is controlled from this desk. A telephone call and it will be delivered.'

'A telephone call?'

'Certainly, you will have a telephone, Mr Carlyle. We understand modern methods.'

'Great,' I said. 'That's marvellous. But we'll cover the orders with chits anyway. I like chits.'

'Certainly, it's best to have proper records.' Mr Tasker thought I was really clever.

We chatted some more and Mr Lott took us to find the machines and meet the drivers. The machines were all right. I couldn't tell yet about the drivers except that one of them looked like an idiot. We let two of them drive the little rear-dumpers out to the site because the rear-dumpers are no more difficult than a lorry, and Dai drove the mover and I took the grab, while the third driver carried Mr Lott in the half-tonner and the fourth came with a five-tonner loaded with stubs and sawn timber and bits and pieces.

I wasn't sure what the security situation was. Papa assured me that Tats were the most honest people in the world, but there's no sense in taking chances, and I wanted to rig up at least a stockade for the vehicles and the drums of oil we would need. Normally I would have spent a long time just working on my own, with Dai, before we bothered about the machinery; but the German survey was fine and only needed checking and there was no sense in spinning out time.

Anyway, the first half-mile was going to be a straightforward business, simply a matter of moving stuff into position, doing a bit of blasting here and there. I worked over it in detail while Dai gave the drivers his crash training course, in which as he always said might not learn to drive well, but they would learn to crash just dandy. Rather than leave the place I told Papa Lott to bring back food and drink from the town in the afternoon, along with his twenty workers if any of them were available. He went off in the big lorry beaming.

When I got hungry out on the track I decided it was time to go back. I work too hard when I get started, and forget about mealtimes and the midday sun, and I was sticky and light in the head when I reached the site. It was seething with bodies.

'What the hell is this?' I asked Dai. 'The chorus of *The Desert Song*?'

He shook his head and said, 'Papa said you gave him the orders, boss, I'm only the cabin-boy.' There must have been sixty apathetic Tats lolling about round the vehicles, and Papa was checking a list in a big black book.

'Here are your workers, Mr Carlyle,' he said proudly.

'I asked for twenty.'

'But they do not work at your wonderful speed, Mr Carlyle.'

'I know, you told me that. I want twenty. That's all.'

He nodded, agreeing with my superior wisdom, and turned and shouted, 'You are too many, nobody wants as many as that! Only twenty. You twenty. The rest go away. Go away!'

The banished Tats looked puzzled and resentful but resigned, and some of them started to pick up jackets and start to walk away.

It was stupid to have gone without food for so long, and work through the noon blaze. If I hadn't been sun-stupid I would have sorted it out very simply, but I got exasperated and shouted at Papa.

'You can't cart forty men out here and then tell them to walk back to Victoria!'

'It's only a few miles, Mr Carlyle. They are strong and healthy.'

'To hell with that. Take them in the truck.'

'The truck is away for more wood, Mr Carlyle.'

'Take them in it when it comes back.'

'You are a thoughtful man, Mr Carlyle.' He turned to the men and shouted, 'You can wait here, Mr Carlyle will allow you to wait here until the truck can take you home. It will only be an hour or two hours.'

'God.' My head was aching. 'What the hell good is that to them?' It wasn't like me. I knew I was known in the trade as the quiet man. It was the sun. 'If the poor bastards are stuck here they may as well work. We need a stockade.'

'You can work!' Papa told them joyfully. 'Mr Carlyle will allow you to work! Come and write your names.'

They all shuffled into a queue and signed their names in Papa's big book, and Dai took me by the elbow and dragged me to a seat in the shade of an overhang.

'Gentle, boss, gentle is what does it,' he crooned. 'You've 'ad a touch of the sun, boy. Give the mighty intellect a bit of peace for a minute and have a chic-ken boy, an' a glass of Tatra Beaujolais, it tastes like boiled celluloid—no, you'd better 'ave a glass of lemonade instead.'

He gave me a little boiled chicken and I tore it up and chewed it and drank the lemonade, out of patience with Tatra and Papa Lott and myself and feeling quite groggy.

'You'll get the better of 'im in the end, boss,' Dai assured me comfortably. 'You 'ave the stayin' power, but you been too long in the sun, boy, you want to lie down for 'alf an hour while I flog the peasants.'

I did, and felt angry and self-justifying. Everybody in Tatra slept for an hour after lunch, and the peasants had already done that before I even saw them. I woke up feeling all right and got in among them with Dai to get the stockade up. The workers were all right. They weren't like lightning

46

and some of them were completely handless, but they were willing enough as long as Dai stormed among them and showed them and laughed at them and pushed them, and when I started heaving timber with my own hands they were startled and overawed. I wondered if Tat protocol strictly forbade bosses to use their muscles like proles, but on the site I was king and made my own protocol, and I could lift a hell of a lot of timber. The boys fell over themselves to show they were stronger than the boss. The old simple tricks always work.

'You done enough, boy,' Dai muttered to me. 'All right, you've proved you're a big boy, now take a rest, you're lookin' as green as Llewellyn's valley.'

'I have an interesting natural pallor,' I snarled at him. 'All right, boy, you're the man with the whip. I'll look at the rocks.'

'John boy, this isn't old Lancashire, you gotto be careful of that ole debbil sun. John. Boy.'

'Sentimental Welsh git,' I said. 'I'll take a stroll instead.'

I looked at the rocks anyway. I felt all right, and I got interested and got as much shade as I could. I made a note in my book to get an aerosol can of orange paint to mark blasting points—the kind of can the Boka fans used.

When I got back the stockade was there. And the mob of workers were shuffling into a queue again.

'What's up?' I asked Papa. 'Do they want you to kiss them good night?'

'Pay,' he said. 'They are queueing for their pay, Mr Carlyle.'

'By the day?' I hadn't thought of that.

'It is no worry, Mr Carlyle, Papa is here to take care of the details. I have enough money.'

I prevented myself from blowing up. I gave him a curt upper-class nod and said, 'Right, carry on.'

'Take it easy, boss, take it easy,' Dai told me. He fell

into step with me on the way to the half-tonner. 'We're in a godless foreign land. We will tame them.'

'You don't seem surprised,' I accused him.

'I met a lot of district councillors in my youth, in the exotic old Rhondda Valley—I got a champion nose for a fiddle.'

'This isn't a flabby democracy,' I reminded him. 'You don't expect corruption with a general in charge and the government organised like an army camp.'

'Were you ever in the Army, boy?' Dai laughed at my innocence. 'Power is the corruption, boy, power, and the greater the power, the louder the fiddle. He's a nice little man, Papa Lott, you don't expect him to sweat all day without taking care of his old age.'

'He won't have any old age if he isn't careful.'

'I don't like to hear you talkin' violent, boss, it isn't your style, you can't go about shootin' people because they might be cookin' the books. A simple kick up the backside is sufficient.'

We got Papa Lott sorted out, I think. I drew enough on the company account to take over all the business of paying the men every day; and Dai was right as usual about corruption. Papa nearly ruptured himself trying to get me to pass this tedious chore down to him. I didn't waste any time on him.

'There is the matter of the deduction for the employment tax,' he bleated.

'How much?'

Papa hesitated and then said, 'Fifteen per cent.'

'I'll make out a daily cheque for it.'

'It is not necessary, Mr Carlyle! I can deposit it with the Ministry, eh? I know the procedure, it makes everything simple.'

'A cheque.'

Papa knew when he was blocked.

I wasn't angry or surprised any longer. I was careful not to work like a maniac in the midday sun and I was past my unnecessary sunstroke and I was in charge of the job. It didn't concern me one way or the other if Lott, or Tasker, or everybody else on the island, was cutting a slice out of the contract. But nobody was going to cut it over my signature.

'There is also the matter of my salary, Mr Carlyle.' The poor little man was getting frantic, and I wondered how the German company had handled him.

'How much?'

I saw Dai turning away to hide a grin. Maybe Dai knew more about me than I did. I never *felt* like a stubborn man. But I couldn't do a job any other way than my own. Papa Lott was grimacing and nodding and trying to soften me with meaningless smiles, to dissolve my stiff-necked British naivete.

'It is more of a commission,' he burbled. 'You understand, Mr Carlyle, that is how things have always arranged themselves, I didn't invent the system.'

'Commission?' I asked him, and nodded to reassure him that this was all right. 'On the output?'

'. . . On the wages.' It was agony for him to get this out.

'I'll take care of it,' I comforted him, and I started to doodle with great concentration till he despaired and walked out of the little hut we were now using as headquarters. Dai and I looked at each other, and I lifted the telephone and got straight through to Tasker. I didn't waste any time on him either.

'The wages,' I said. 'I'm paying them daily. I propose to get a signature from each of the men for the net amount and send you a copy every day. Will you pay the employment tax direct to the Ministry?'

'The employment tax . . .' I could suddenly visualise

Tasker doing a series of little contortions like Lott's. 'Yes . . . Let me think about it, Mr Carlyle.'

'Right,' I said. 'If you like, I'll do it myself. By cheque. Either way you please, Mr Tasker. Then there's Mr Lott's salary. You could work out his commission from your wage sheets and pay him. Or I'll do it if you like. By cheque.'

There was a silence of some seconds, and then Tasker said, 'Of course, of course, Mr Carlyle. I didn't expect to concern myself with these details, but if you feel you have too much office work . . .'

'No, I haven't. I'll do it if you like. By cheque.'

'Yes . . . I can work something out, of course. Oh.' This was in the tone of a sudden casual afterthought. 'I wanted to speak to Mr Lott about something else. Is he there?'

I decided not to be so cruel as to sit in the office while Papa talked to his boss. He was petrified enough without that. Dai and I went out, and Dai started to teach a beefy big Tat how to use a pick. I noticed something familiar about a slim labourer filling a wheelbarrow and working harder at it than the average Tat. When I stared at him he turned to face me, grinning without shame. It was the ukelele player.

'What the hell are you doing here?' I asked him.

'Working, boss.'

'Don't call me boss.'

'I can work, I'm okay.' He proved it by getting dug in with the shovel. I stopped him and grabbed his wrist. He was wearing a numbered plastic disc on a chain. That should have been all right, it was our own system. Every man had a numbered disc so that there would be no nonsense about passers-by wandering into the pay line. But I had taken a good look at all the workers the day before, and I would have recognised the ukelele player.

'What's your name?'

'Martin.'

'You weren't here yesterday.'

'Lucas was here yesterday, I'm here today, what's the problem?'

'Does Lucas come back tomorrow?'

He shrugged cheerfully. 'Maybe Lucas, maybe Harry, what's the problem? Who wants to work every day? Work to sustain life is a part of life. Work to gather property is a part of death.'

'Boka he say.'

'That's right, boss.'

'Don't call me boss.'

'Twenty shillings. It's enough. Everybody eats.'

'Is it a big family?' I didn't care about this kind of deception, as long as all his brothers worked as hard as he did.

'No, just the gang,' he said. 'So what's a family? Mankind is a family. Embracing womankind.' He giggled.

'If Boka he say that he's been plagiarising Joe Miller,' I said. 'Does Boka work?'

'Boka works.'

'It's none of my business.'

'Thanks, boss.' I couldn't be angry with the pup, he was too cheerful. I wondered if Papa Lott was a fan of Boka's, but it seemed too bizarre.

When I whistled for wage call and paid the men I noticed that Papa Lott was smartly in the truck cab with the first passenger load back to town. He and Tasker would no doubt work out a new system of carving up the commission now that I had made my position clear, and they were welcome. I noticed Martin the ukelele boy waving to the other men and setting off on his own, off the road and towards the little cluster of white houses about a mile across the plain. Dai was out checking the equipment and counting shovels, and the last truckload was away, when the telephone rang in the hut. It was Tasker's secretary, with a message that Sir Malcolm would like Mr Carlyle and Mr Owen to

visit him for dinner. It sounded like a good idea, but I said
I would call back because I wanted to make sure that Dai
hadn't evolved some alternative plan with a bird. He came
back to the hut a few seconds later and said, 'No way of
beatin' the bastards, boy, it's started.'

'Malcolm wants us for dinner tonight,' I said.

He was thrown off his train of thought, and looked
confused for a second.

'No, I don' feel like it, see, boy? Not tonight.'

'We've got to eat,' I said. 'We might as well enjoy it.'

'No, not tonight.'

'Have you found a bird?'

'It's none of your business, I don't feel like goin', that's
all.' It was quite unlike him.

'Don't be daft, we've got nothing else to do.'

'You don't have to go on an' on about it see? If I don't
want to go why don't you bloody well leave me alone?
He's your friend,' he added, half in apology. 'I'm only an
extra man, boy, you go on your own.'

'What the hell's got into you? I thought you liked Myra.'

'I'm a free man, right? I would rather be on my own.
Anyway one of the vibrators is missin', that's what I came
to tell you.'

'Are you sure?'

This was a silly question. Dai was always sure. But
curiously enough this question didn't irritate him at all. He
just shook his head at the absurdity of it and said, 'They're
probably sellin' it in a pub this very minute.'

'Damn,' I said.

'Carried unanimously, boy.'

'Wait a minute,' I said. 'Martin. The ukelele boy. He
walked off that way. He didn't catch the truck. Maybe he's
got it hidden somewhere for picking up.'

'Ah, they're a funny crowd, that mob,' Dai said. 'I was
just goin' to tell you, there's seven of them with a job

among them, I would have thrown him out if he hadn't been workin' so hard.'

'Damn,' I said. I hesitated for a second and then picked up the telephone and told Tasker's secretary to let Sir Malcolm know that we were going to be working late at the site and wouldn't manage for dinner. Dai looked away while I was talking.

'Do you not like Malcolm?' I asked him, unable to leave it alone, and he said:

'He's all right, I just don't feel sociable, leave it at that, boss.'

'Okay.'

We left the half-tonner in the compound, but we checked everything and for the first time took off rotor arms and locked them in the office.

'Why would anybody want a vibrator?' Dai wondered, and I said:

'Maybe they're using it instead of bongo drums.'

It was still light, but there wasn't much left of the day. We took a sight on the hamlet and started to walk. Dai insisted on bringing crash helmets, and he had a tyre lever in the long foot-rule pocket of his trousers. It was wise enough. Anybody resolute enough to steal something as heavy as a vibrator might be resolute enough to defend his capture.

A score of houses had been flung down on either side of a stream among growing maize, and fig palms seemed to be growing where they chose. Blue darkness settled round us as we crossed the plain under a sliver of moon. The smell of mimosa made it even cornier.

'Why would anybody in a place like this want a vibrator?' Dai was baffled and angry, and added, 'Why would they want a bloody road either? They got everythin', boy, every mortal thing.'

'Like dry lavatories?'

'You always want jam on it, boss.'

53

'We don't know anything,' I said. 'Maybe Papa Lott has the vibrator in his briefcase.'

'Don't think I haven't thought of that, boss, I'm not just two pretty faces.'

Of course, as we approached the hamlet we realised we didn't know what we were going to do. We could hardly go round knocking on all the doors and asking for a stolen vibrator. The villagers might even be the kind of people who shot strangers on sight.

But we didn't have to decide. Somebody started to light smudge-pots near the river a couple of hundred yards away, and somebody else lit lanterns hanging from palms.

'They're getting ready for us,' Dai muttered.

'It's a wedding. It must be a wedding.'

We sat down by the river, invisible in the dark, and watched. It was clearly a wedding.

'Maybe that's what they want the vibrator for,' I said, and Dai said:

'I was just goin' to say the same thing, you got a horrible dirty mind, boy.' We sat for some minutes, and then he said, 'You're right, boss, it's embarrassin', isn't it? We got no business here.'

'I enjoyed the walk,' I said. We got up to go, but somebody shouted at us from the darkness, and when we didn't answer, trotted towards us.

'It's the Welshman,' he said. It was the fat boy we had given a lift with the crowd of Beautiful People. 'You're in time for the feast,' he said.

'We just came to look, boy, we're goin'.'

'It's free!' The kid couldn't understand anybody who turned down free food. 'They feed anybody at a wedding. Come on. Hey, Martin! It's the Welshman!'

Martin came out of the dark carrying his ukelele and said hello and said, 'It's all right, you can come, it's my cousin's wedding.'

'We were just passing.' I put on the boss image, but Dai was interested. He said:

'It's a bit of education, isn't it? There might be a few birds.' Crude sod.

Martin laughed and said, 'I don't know if there's any old enough for you.'

'Any bird would rather have a man, boy, than a little boy, even with a ukelele,' Dai said, and they both laughed. They understood each other. Maybe there's an international brotherhood of peasants.

We were pushed towards the wedding, and the kid Martin tried to introduce us, but everybody was waiting for the ukelele music, and we found ourselves standing alone while people started to dance. It was too complicated for me, a cross between Greek dancing and an eightsome reel, and the music, from the ukelele and a concertina, was a funny mixture too, Turkish-flavoured French. The men wore black and most of the girls wore white, but the lads kept their tee-shirts and jeans. Dai got in among it at once. No sense of decorum.

A bony old boy with a face like a Welsh mine came and gave me a glass of lime juice and sat beside me and said, 'You are Martin's friend.'

'I work on the road,' I defended myself.

He shook his head and said, 'A bad boy. He will be the death of his mother my sister.'

An equally bony woman, this one in black, sat at my other side, hot and flushed, and said, 'He is young, he's young, leave him alone.' Dai was enlivening the dance with the maniac shrieks of wild Welsh Wales.

'No discipline, no respect for authority,' the old man pronounced. 'Boka, Boka, nobody but Boka he listens to.'

'Boka is a good boy,' the woman insisted. 'Give the man a glass of wine, lime juice is for the children.'

'There is too much wine-drinking,' the old boy said

darkly, and went to fetch me a beaker of the familiar boiled-celluloid Tatra brew.

'He thinks everybody should be as sad as himself,' the woman said tolerantly. 'The young have learned better, they are learning how to be happy.'

'Where is their religion?' the old boy demanded, and she answered comfortably:

'They will come back to religion, there are plenty of good Christians who would steal your false leg and still look holy.'

'I have no false leg,' he said flatly, 'so how can anybody steal it?'

'I am lucky to have a man with five sound limbs,' she laughed, and he lowered his brows at her, but she made a little gesture towards him with her hand and said again, 'I am lucky,' and he grunted some kind of reluctant forgiveness, and said:

'Boka, Boka, they listen to nobody but Boka.'

'You don't want to hear our quarrels,' the woman said to me, 'they are for our own amusement. You are making the road.' Everybody knew everything, of course.

'I have nothing against Boka,' the old boy muttered, 'but there is no discipline.'

'Nothing against Boka, nothing against Boka,' his wife sang. 'He is like a boy when Boka visits us, he is like a child waiting for Boka to make him laugh.'

'I do not laugh,' the old boy protested, and the woman told me confidentially:

'He is ashamed to laugh, it's against the old religion, if our grandfathers never laughed we should never laugh. I wish I was seventeen, I would laugh.'

'No religion,' the old man persisted. 'He should have more respect.'

'Dance with me, sad man,' she said to him. 'You are too young to be sad.' She dragged him to his feet, and when she put her arms round him she squeezed him hard and he looked embarrassed and nearly happy. There was a vast earthenware bowl on one of the tables, full of lime juice. I caught the fat boy hovering over it, and he started guiltily when I came up behind him, but when he recognised me he giggled, and whipped a gallon jug from under the table and started to empty it into the lime juice.

'It's too draggy,' he explained. 'We got to get it off the ground.' He splashed the last inch of the stuff in the jug into two glasses and gave me one. I took a mouthful and it tasted like water. Then it burst into flames halfway to my stomach. He looked into my face, waiting for the reaction, and sniggered in delight. I shook my head and walked on. Martin and the concertina player were still working away and Dai was in the middle of the dance measuring and weighing the birds.

Half out of the ring of light, a number of children were squatting round a short, very squat young man in his twenties. He had a broad-boned face and a broken nose and he was doing an act for them.

'. . . so the princess held the golden coin as tight as she could so that she could keep it for ever . . .' he was saying, and he had a penny in his hand. He closed his fingers and then peered into his closed fist. He was a good children's entertainer, very serious and very funny, and he used his face to tell the next bit of the story and then opened his empty hand and sniffed all over it for the missing penny and was stupefied when it turned up in his other hand.

'. . . every time she wanted it, it slipped away. But when she didn't need it, it turned up everywhere. . .' He found it in his ear and in his hair and then in his mouth, couldn't get it out and swallowed it. The kids squealed in horror and delight till he wrenched it out of his stomach.

'So what is the good of a gold coin that only makes me sick, the princess thought. I was happier before I found it.

57

And she *threw* it away.' This scandalised the kids. Kids don't like throwing money away. He swung his arm back and threw it over their heads and clutched a poppy out of the air.

'Who wants a lousy old coin anyway?' he protested. 'At least you can smell a flower. Have a flower,' he added to a small girl at the front. She held out her hand and the flower and a penny dropped into it.

'Show us, Boka, show us!' a small boy screamed. The squat man laughed and produced another penny and held out his hand and rolled it across the back of his knuckles and they crowded round to watch the magic exposed. He glanced over their heads and caught my eye and tilted his head and hunched his shoulders and laughed and said, 'It's better than working, isn't it?' I laughed in return without knowing why. It was typical of Tatra, I thought. The patron saint was a conjurer. We were never going to track down the missing vibrator, even if we had the bad taste to try, in the middle of a wedding feast. Wedding guests nodded to me, friendly enough but not forthcoming. The feast was a table not unlike a conventional buffet with piles of vegetables and fruit and bowls of hot sauce and sticks with little bits of meat and stuff skewered along them.

I sat down beside Dai and warned him off the lime juice, but he wasn't interested.

'I am number fourteen in the queue for a dance with the bride,' he said proudly. 'I'm right in 'ere, boy, I got this genius for mixin' with the natives, see? I'm a proper white-haired boy, I am, but the girls are terrible respectable, terrible respectable.'

'Is that bad?' I asked him.

'No, no, now you come to mention it the hottest girls I ever met in Cardiff was all Salvation Army, but the worst you could get from them was an old tambourine across your head, when you're abroad you never know if they might go in for something more along the lines of a bayonet or a poisoned brick or somethin' if you go too fast, boy.'

I saw the groom, sweating and embarrassed in a good black suit and being teased by his lewd friends; and the bride, a thin little thing also sweating in white and dancing with a middle-aged man. As she left his arms, one of the groom's pals suddenly remembered his privilege and was making for her. A man in olive green with knee-high boots grabbed her, and the boy froze in mid-stride. There was one of those little ripples of silence spreading out from the dancing pair, suddenly. People turned to look, and then looked away.

'Policeman's privileges?' I asked Dai.

'Pig's privileges,' he said. The other dancers were avoiding the policeman and the bride so carefully that a wide space formed round them and they were dancing alone. The policeman looked round as he danced, happy and challenging. He was holding the little girl with more enthusiasm and freedom than most people would show in public with anybody's wife. I looked at the groom, a skinny boy of twenty. He was white, and his friends were trying not to look at him. The boy who had been going to dance with the bride made a worthy attempt at smoothing the problem out by going forward and tapping the policeman politely on the shoulder. The cop swung his fist back without looking round, and the boy ducked it and backed away.

'I think number fourteen's come up.' Dai started to rise but I gripped his arm and said:

'You're not going to help anybody if you start a fight.'

'All right,' Dai muttered, 'I'll give him three minutes.'

Something or nothing was going to happen, but the policeman was really going too far. Having dismissed the boy so easily, he laughed round at everybody and shouted, 'A bride needs a real man to teach her, eh?' He put his hands over the girl's buttocks and gripped them and lifted

59

her clear of the ground. It was no longer a dance, but a fertility ritual. The ukelele and the concertina stopped. The bride started to whimper as she was jogged up and down.

A voice in the crowd cut into the thick silence.

'Your arm will heal. Don't worry.'

Boka walked out and stood facing the policeman over the bride's head, and pointing at the man's right arm. The policeman paused and glared at him and said, 'What arm? I have two good arms.'

Boka stared back at him and said gently, 'You have lost the power of your arm. It is common. The muscles have frozen. It is common. The fingers are dead. It is common. The shoulder is paralysed. It is common. The elbow is stiff like wood. It is common. It will heal.'

It was all familiar. I've seen an American woman doing it in cabaret, and it was the sheer speed of it that startled me then too because I had always thought that hypnotists had to go on endlessly making magic passes and shining torches into their victim's eyes. The policeman kept glaring at Boka, but the fingers of his right hand opened out and went stiff. The aah sound from the guests was very quiet. The policeman forgot the bride and stared at his arm, and she slipped out of his grasp and ran to her husband.

'What are you playing at?' the policeman roared, and began to fumble across his body to open his pistol holster. Boka held out a hand, and the policeman's groping arm fell to his side. Fear started to edge the anger from his face,

'It's paralysed,' he muttered. 'My arm! You've poisoned me.'

Boka shook his head.

'It is the night air of the district. It is common. You already felt it on your way here. It is common.' The policeman thought hard and nodded, yes, he had felt it on his way.

'You a doctor?' he asked thickly.

Boka took the paralysed arm by the wrist without answering and said, 'There may be a stiffness also in the right leg. It is common. It will heal. You must keep it moving, till you can rest in bed.' He began to lead the policeman like an obedient dog across the ring of light, gently kneading the man's wrist. They passed out of the light and into the darkness. The aah sound was louder this time. The father of the bride was standing behind me.

'He knew. He could see that the arm was paralysed before the policeman felt it. He has sharp eyes.'

'It was a punishment from God,' his wife said with a trace of hysteria, and she appealed to me. 'Was it not a punishment from God?'

'It was a nice neat . . .' I looked at her, as she nodded in angry satisfaction that there was justice under God, and I shut up and nodded and then said, 'It looked like it.'

The ukelele boy started to strum furiously, and after a pause the skinny boy grabbed the bride and started to dance. I could feel Dai unstiffening and unclenching his fists. The demonstration had been so fast that I still had my restraining hand on him.

'Boka would make a good foreman,' I said.

'A bit of the old magic, boy, I could do with a bit of that old stuff. Will he have to walk home? Serve him bloody right.'

The father said sullenly, 'No, they always leave their motor-cycles in the distance, to come quietly on foot.'

'What for?' His wife still had the edge of hysteria in her voice. 'What badness can they find here? We have no time to be thieves or murderers, we work too hard to have time for trouble.'

'If you got cops, missus, you got trouble,' Dai told her, and she nodded in violent agreement and patted his shoulder. Above the sound of the music I heard the kick kick and roar of a big two-stroke, and I hoped the cop was driving off with the hounds of hell at his heels. When Boka came back a few minutes later people crowded round him, but he smiled and waved them aside and they respectfully left him alone. I would have done the same, but a little later he came and sat beside me.

'It was a good trick,' I said. He nodded ruefully, and I added 'My friend would probably have knocked his head off.'

'Yes,' he said. 'Violence breeds violence—the clichés are always true. People would rather have tricks than the truth,' he added sadly.

'You're not fooling anybody,' I said. 'You enjoy your tricks.'

He kept on shaking his head sadly, but then smiled and then laughed, a round bass noise. 'I don't fool myself. You're right. We're all actors.' Dai whirled past with the bride in his arms and gave Boka the thumbs-up sign. 'The curiosity matters,' Boka said. 'If you're not curious about little things like tricks you're not curious about big things, the energy source is the same. You're the road man.'

'How can I deny it? Everybody in Tatra knows everything.'

'Do they? I know nearly nothing. Were you curious to see a native wedding?'

'No,' I said. 'Dai and I were looking for a vibrator somebody stole.'

'Valuable?'

'Very.'

He nodded and said, 'There will always be theft, it's childish to believe that man can outgrow all their illnesses. They can try, maybe that's enough.'

'You don't know anything about the vibrator?'

'Me? What could I do with a vibrator? Is it useful?'

'For breaking rocks, yes, it's very useful.'

'I'm a very indolent man.' He laughed.

'Would any of your boys have stolen it?'

'No.' He was quite firm. 'We will steal a fish from the river. Or an apple. We have no morals.' He giggled. 'Can you eat a vibrator?'

'Do you know of anybody else who might?'

'Anybody. Your men work for money. Some of them must be greedy.'

'Anybody else?'

'There are weak men everywhere.' He turned an open, blank, candid face to me.

'What do your boys *do*?' I was really curious. He tried to understand the question, and said:

'They are not my boys. I don't own anybody. They call me a leader or something. It's silly. Everybody has to lead himself. But they're indolent, like me, only I think faster, so they let me think a lot. What do we do? We eat and talk, and chase birds.'

The modern slang was like a jolt, and he saw it, because he laughed and said, 'Your own Dr Johnson said that there are few ways in which a man can be more innocently employed than in committing adultery in his mind.'

'I thought you were going to say than in getting money.'

Boka giggled.

'I know, he said that too. I'm inconsistent too. Sex is a curse. It's a slave-driver and a destroyer. I'm resigned to liking it when I can get it for all that.'

'The day we arrived in Tatra,' I said, 'somebody rolled a boulder at us. It might have killed us. Could that have been your boys?'

'What for?' He was astonished. 'Kill an animal, and you become an animal. Not that you are an animal. Why do you dislike me?'

'I don't,' I said. 'I just don't want to like you without knowing more about you.'

'It's one way,' he agreed. 'I find it easier to like everybody and find out about them later.'

'And then hate them.'

'No. People are what they are, you have to love them for what they are. We are not God, to hate a man because he doesn't fit the scene we've invented. He has his own scene, he's the hero in his own movie. He might be right.'

'Who is it that throws boulders at tourists?' I hung on to this rather than be diverted with his bits of philosophy. He gave me the blank candid look again.

'If a country is angry at the top it will be angry at the bottom.'

'Revolutionaries?' I asked him.

'We are all revolutionaries.'

'If you knew, would you tell?'

'That's a nice problem of conscience, isn't it? Would I help the police to catch a revolutionary? Would I help a revolutionary to kill a policeman?'

I became aware that for the last few minutes a girl had been sitting on the other side of me, and when she saw that I had noticed her she said, 'Don't stop, I like dialogue.'

'My sister. Marie,' Boka said.

'John Carlyle.'

'I know,' she said. 'If you've stopped talking you can dance with me.' Boka laughed, and I got up and we danced. The space between the tables was crowded and the dance could be nothing more than a rudimentary polka. It had got very very noisy. The father of the bride cannoned into us and apologised, swayed beside us and said slurrily, 'The lime juice is bewitched.' When Marie laughed a trilling laugh he looked vaguely suspicious and said, 'Has Boka bewitched the lime juice?' I heard the words being repeated among the dancers. Some of them stopped and grabbed cups to dip in the punchbowl. Others kept dancing and laughed knowingly. The young kids started to burrow their way through to the table to try the bewitched lime juice.

'Everybody blames Boka,' Marie laughed up at me. She wasn't slim but she wasn't fleshy either. Strong thick bones.

'He asks for it,' I said.

'Oo, oo, moral rectitude.' She laughed again, a mother jollying her child out of a tantrum. 'Drink some lime juice, John Carlyle, your square shoes are showing.'

'Would you like some?'

'I don't need it, I'm self-generating.'

I forgot about Boka and concentrated on the girl, and looked right into her eyes, half analysing and half challenging. She looked right back and shook her head and laughed again.

'Call off the sex war, I'm not your enemy.' She had too damned much motherly understanding. 'I'm dancing with you, did you notice?'

Dai bumped into us, clutching a lassie with a Nefertiti profile and a dim expression.

'About time too, boy,' he yelled above the noise. 'I'm halfway there.'

Marie chuckled as we shuffled about, and said, 'Is *he* in for a disappointment!'

'Why? Do girls in Tatra not go?'

She gave me that look again and said, 'Are we opening hostilities again?'

'I only asked a simple question.'

'No question is simple. Boka he say.' We both laughed. She had it, you know, the quality, she seemed absolutely sure of herself and happy with it. It doesn't matter what they look like if they have that. I've sometimes thought that when I got really hungry for a particular girl it was because unconsciously I envied what she had, beauty or grace or happiness or even an interesting kind of misery, and I imagined that by getting hold of her I could steal whatever it was for myself. I don't mean that Marie was ugly or even very plain, though I wasn't particularly noticing the shape of her face. She was all right, but if she had looked like the back end of a camel this kind of arrogant serenity would still have shone through and made me want to steal it.

'I withdraw the question,' I said. She squeezed my arm momentarily, in sympathy I suppose, and pointed her face up and I kissed her quickly on the lips and she smiled, but not as if it meant anything.

'I like you,' I said. She chuckled.

'You mean you would like a quick roll.'

'I mean that too.' I laughed. 'Is that the way girls talk in Tatra?'

Her laughter pealed. 'You're jesting! We're the original formalised society, man. And, anyway, not tonight.'

'I like you, I'm not lying,' I said.

'I like you too.'

'It sounds like a good arrangement. You might enjoy it.'

'I would, I would.' She kept on laughing, and then said sternly, 'But it would be bad for you.'

'Let me worry about that, you don't have to care.'

'Even hating is better than not caring,' she chastened me. 'Boka he say.'

'Oh, I like you, John Carlyle.'

'Great, just great.'

But she made me laugh, anyway. I could have killed her. On the way back to town we saw the flashing light of another road block ahead.

'That is all we need, boy,' Dai said bitterly. 'A brush-off and then a beating-up. If I have one wrong word from a Gestapo man I'll let my hormones go berserk and strangle him. Or rape him?' I pulled up at the block and a policeman came forward with torch shining.

'Mr Carlyle?' he asked respectfully, and I nodded, and

he said, 'Thank you, sir, we were asked to look out for you. Sir Malcolm was worried when you didn't return to your hotel.'

'Oh. We were working late,' I said lamely.

'Quite all right, sir, as long as you're all right, sir.' He saluted smartly and went aside to let us through.

'Very helpful,' I muttered. 'We should have asked him if he could supply us with a couple of birds.'

'Ach, man, I'm off birds for life,' said Dai. 'I've a good mind to take up knittin', there's no nasty disappointments in knittin'.'

'See if you can knit a spare vibrator,' I said, and he said:

'I could, too, if you give me the right kind of wool.' But he laughed. In a way, the big let-down with a girl can be more entertaining than a big success. However, when he came into the site hut in the middle of the following morning he was looking quite unfunny. He eased a wooden box off his shoulder and dumped it on my desk and said:

'Neat, boy, neat, I would never have noticed it till we wanted it.' He pointed to the padlock and touched it, and it swung free. He lifted it off and opened the box.

'Never mind the vibrator, boy, we've lost enough dynamite to turn the government palace into confetti.'

'Coloured confetti?' I asked him. 'Coloured confetti is my favourite.'

5

WE were dishonest about it.
'It's our own damned fault,' I said, and Dai said:
'My own damned fault.'

'Our own damned fault. I'll have to get through on the hot line and tell Tasker to call the police. We can report the vibrator at the same time.'

'That's right, boss.'

He stood, and I sat, for several seconds.

'But you're not in a hurry to call the police,' Dai said.

'We'll have to.'

'I know.' Another pause. 'But you're not in a hurry.'

'They'll come out here and question the men. They'll probably beat them up . . .'

'. . . or maybe shoot a few to encourage them, boy.'

'I wish to hell you wouldn't call me boy. Damn and blast. They'll turn the damn site upside down and find nothing.'

'And I'll take a punch at one of them when he's only doin' his job, proddin' his bayonet up my backside . . .'

'. . . and we'll get ten years in jail.'

'With rats and lice, boy, don' forget the rats and lice.'

'Damn.'

'And blast.'

'Yes.'

'I am a raving idiot, boss, the stuff was safe enough

locked up in the compound but dynamite is never safe enough. I'll bring the rest in here.'

'The other thing you'll do is make screw-up shutters for the insides of these windows. That won't stop the bastards from burning the hut down,' I added glumly. Dai was glad to be doing something other than standing cursing himself. He went to work. I made up my mind that I wouldn't phone Tasker, but see Malcolm and get his advice before I did anything. I could say that I had just discovered both thefts and had come straight to him.

'It nearly looks as if we were takin' sides,' Dai said.

'I'm not taking the side of any bastard who wants to blow people up. I'm just trying to minimise the trouble. Will you come along to Malcolm's when we finish?'

He started to shake his head, and then said, 'All right, boy, I can back you up an' act a bit hysterical while you talk nice and calm and authoritative.'

We overtook the last truckload of workers on the way to town and drove straight to the pink house. The streets were nearly deserted, but we saw five police trucks moving about and there were twelve or more policemen hovering about in front of the government palace. Dai and I looked at each other and I knew he was wondering too if the dynamite had been used already. When we got to Malcolm's there was a policeman guarding the wrought-iron gate, and he asked for our names and rang the bell himself. Myra came to the front door and waved, and the cop let us into the garden. She was just as twitchy as she had been the first time.

'Hello, John. Hello . . . Dai, isn't it?'

'Yes, ma'am,' said Dai.

She kept looking away from us as she spoke.

'There's been some trouble—you'd better see Malcolm, I suppose, if it's urgent—he's very busy.'

'It's urgent,' I said.

She showed us through the house to Malcolm's study. He had just finished telephoning, and he drummed his fingers on his desk without getting up.

'Sorry, lads,' he said, 'I'm rather preoccupied—nice to see you, all the same. Bad trouble, I'm afraid.'

There were three telephones on the desk, and a long intercom box with twenty buttons. The intercom crackled and said, 'Section three. Suspects four. Material negative.'

Malcolm drew a line through a square on the street map in front of him and flipped a switch and said, 'Hold section three. Unit five, move through section two and check with unit one before moving into section five. Unit one will take section four. But rendezvous first so that nobody can slip back.' He moved a poker chip across the map and looked up and said, 'Not very sophisticated but it works.'

My heart sank. I was convinced that the dynamite had already been used.

'Are you in charge of the police?' Dai asked in wonderment.

'No. Co-ordinating.' Malcolm was crisp and very much in command. 'The dock warehouse was broken into last night. Three cases of dynamite are missing.'

'My God!' I didn't look at Dai and he didn't look at me, but we both knew what we were thinking and we were both delighted. It was a shame about the warehouse dynamite, but I wasn't going to gain anything by bleating about our dynamite, and I didn't intend to, and Dai knew it.

One of the phones rang, and Malcolm listened and said, 'Four. Three. Six. Keep in touch,' and slammed down the receiver and said to me, 'What's your trouble? Sorry, John, but I am up to the ears in this, it's a crisis.'

'We lost a vibrator,' I said. 'Or maybe it was stolen. Or mislaid. It doesn't matter, I can cope.'

He made notes on the edge of the street map.

'You're lucky you got here without being stopped,' he said.

'And beaten up?' Dai asked innocently.

'I've advised them to avoid violence, unnecessary violence. It's inefficient. Unfortunately I don't control the police, I'm only commissioned to reorganise their strategy.'

'Police? That's a new lark for you,' I said.

'Administration is administration.' He smiled quite happily. 'If you can administer a farm or a boot factory you can administer anything else. Work study applies to police forces as well as food distribution. Yes?' He picked up the ringing phone again. 'No, wait till section five arrives.' He put the phone down.

'You'd better wait till this blows over and then you can have help to find the vibrator, whatever it is, John. In the meantime, I would be glad, honestly, if you would stick to your job and don't get involved in other things. You know what I mean.'

'No, I don't.'

'An officer reports that you obstructed him in the performance of his duty,' Malcolm said. 'Understandable if you thought he was too enthusiastic, and perhaps unintentional. But this isn't Birmingham or Yorkshire. And how in heaven's name did you get mixed up with the Boka gang?'

'Mixed up?'

'The police may be a bit rough at the edges, but they know what goes on, John. I'm not blaming you for being curious about the natives, but a thing like this is very embarrassing to me.'

'I met him by accident,' I said. 'He seems a decent enough kid.'

'We were looking for the vibrator,' Dai said.

'It's all right, I know how these things happen, but this dynamite business puts everything in a different light. Don't go near any of these odd bods from now on. Not that

71

it's likely,' he added. 'They should all be rounded up before very long.'

'What for?'

'Don't be naive, John. There's a good government here, if it gets a chance. But it's still unsure of itself and it's military by training, and when somebody's roaming the island with a heap of dynamite the General obviously takes the military line. Strike first.'

'But Boka doesn't believe in violence,' I persisted.

'Maybe he doesn't. I might have been interested in debating it yesterday. Now we can't afford to take chances and we can't afford any hysterical personality cults. A lot of people take your Boka for some kind of prophet of God. That spells trouble.'

'He's only a tubby wee man who doesn't like working,' I protested.

'Ha! Turning lime juice into wine! Curing the paralysed! I've got a dossier on him this thick. Walking on water too, I wouldn't be surprised. He's a smelly little peasant with a Christ-complex.'

'Maybe Christ was a bit smelly like too,' Dai said mildly, and Malcolm's brow came down in disapproval and he ignored Dai and said:

'We've got a great social experiment in the making here and it needs a chance, it needs peace to work. Hello?' Another of the telephones was ringing.

As he lifted it I said, 'Good night, then,' and turned to go. He waved a friendly hand and got back to business. I was angry. I was halfway down the drive and about to say something to Dai when I realised I had walked out without him. I turned back and he trotted out of the front door to join me.

'What the hell kept you?' I demanded.

'Don't work it out on me, boy, I got shorter legs than you have. He's crackin' efficient, isn't he?'

'He's got his job to do.'

'He's welcome to mine too, he's got so many he probably wouldn't notice. I feel like goin' back to Liverpool, personally.'

It was so near to what I was thinking that I was irritated, and said, 'We'll finish the job.' Dai shrugged

Even the Hotel Louis was a bit electric, though we got there without actually being beaten up. We went to the bar and found a woman serving, rather inefficiently considering there was nobody there but us. 'Is it Charles's night off?' I asked her.

She faltered and said, 'Charles is . . . He has gone to the police station . . . to help.'

I didn't know whether that meant Charles was a police spy or whether he had been taken for a bashing in the cells. 'Give me a bottle of Scotch,' I said. 'Put it on my bill.' While she was wondering whose bill that meant, I picked up the bottle and we went to my suite. I bolted the door.

'We never had this trouble in Manchester, boy,' Dai said. He kicked off his shoes and pulled off his socks and lay on the floor.

I thought I had left a glass in the bedroom and went to look for it. 'Dai!' I called. He came in. Somebody had been crudely searching the bedroom. The drawers were open, and stuff, the very small amount of stuff I travelled with, was scattered on the floor.

'They're after us, boy,' Dai said calmly.

'The stupid bastards are probably searching everywhere. No bloody idea,' I said. I started to go into the bathroom. There was a resistance against the door. I got angry and heaved it open.

A man in jeans and a dark suit was flung back inside the bathroom and I was ready to punch him when he said, 'They're after me.'

'Who are you?'

'Nobody, they're picking up everybody. Sorry to intrude,' he added, with a touch of spurious jauntiness.

'Are you another of Boka's boys?' Dai demanded.

The man shrugged his shoulders at so obvious a deduction, and Dai said, 'Well, get to hell out of here.'

'Right to hell,' I said. 'I don't want to know about it. You can get over the garden wall,' I added.

'Thank you, sir,' the man said. 'Sorry to have disturbed you.' He was past us like a flash, through the french windows and into the darkness of the courtyard.

'We're getting to hell too,' I told Dai. 'They can get somebody else to finish the bloody road—there's a dead body in the bath.'

'Anybody we know?' Dai was too quick to do any double-takes.

He wasn't anybody we knew, but at least he was a civilian, and in a curious way, this was comforting. I tottered to the lavatory bowl and sat on it to concentrate on being frightened.

'What are you thinkin', boss?'

'I'm thinking . . .' My voice was shaky, and I took a grip and started again, 'I'm thinking of Liverpool with the rain lashing down and a plague of rats and the men have just gone on strike and I've broken a leg falling down a sewer. It's lovely.'

'We'd better get the police.'

'Yes. He's dead all right. Stabbed.'

'Oh, God.'

Everything might have been all right, all the same. It was natural, but foolish, to want to keep away from the police in Tatra. The ordinary detective squad might be quite civilised and not given to lashing out with sticks at the first sign of movement. And we were not teenagers or students or peasants, we were very important people with friends in high places. And you can't have a body in the

74

bath and walk about pretending it isn't there. However, at that moment there was a deafening banging on the door of the lounge, and I shot through to answer it and closed the bathroom door and the bedroom door behind me without even thinking why.

There was a wiry customer in the corridor, another civilian, but with that unmistakable look of authority as well as a drawn revolver.

'Police,' he said. 'Is this your room?'

'Yes. I am John Carlyle.'

'I'm looking for a man in a dark suit. Have you seen anybody suspicious?'

And again it might have been all right except that as he spoke he strode into the room and shoved me aside with his shoulder and barked, 'How long have you been in your room? Can you prove your identity?'

'Five minutes,' I said. 'I just came from Sir Malcolm Wreford's house.'

'You know Sir Malcolm Wreford? Is there anybody else here?' He was already barging into the bedroom, and I was going to say no. God knows why I was going to say no except that my instinct was to say no to everything. The toilet flushed noisily and Dai came out of the bathroom zipping up his flies.

'My colleague, Mr Owen,' I said. The cop looked round the mess of drawers and clothes without surprise.

'The french window's open,' I said. 'It was open when we arrived.'

He gave us a hard stare and went back into the lounge and out into the courtyard. He shouted up at somebody in the hotel, holstered his gun and took a running leap at the enclosing wall and pulled himself over and fired his revolver at something and started to run.

'Why didn't you mention the body?' I asked Dai.

'Why didn't you mention the body?' Dai asked me.

'We've scuppered the bloody contract now,' I said. 'We're buggered, in fact.'

'Phone your old Sir Malcolm, boy.'

'Would you?'

'No. We don't want to be an embarrassment, do we?'

'Screw you,' I said.

'Granted, boss.'

6

WHAT seems surprising now is how easily we slipped into a criminal enterprise, the disposal of the body. It was ludicrous that we should be involved in anything so daft when all we had to do was scream for a policeman and show him the stranger in the bath. If he turned out to be a dynamite thief we might even get a medal.

'He isn't a dynamite thief,' I told Dai. 'The other one might be. The only thing that could possibly have happened is that the other bloke was hiding in here, a cop came in to search the place and found him, and that's the cop.'

'We could still report it and look innocent,' Dai said doubtfully.

'You're the lad who hates cops,' I said. 'I don't like this crowd much either. They've practically got us tied up with some big Boka conspiracy already.'

'They couldn't prove it in court.'

'They could make a hell of a mess of us in the meantime.'

'You're the boss, boss,' he said cheerfully.

'Thanks very much, Welsh bastard,' I said. 'You stay with laughing boy and I'll go outside and think of something hopeless.'

I went out, and Dai locked the door behind me. The hotel bar was deserted, and the dining room was deserted. My first hope was the half-tonner. It was there all right, at the front door. But I couldn't see how we could use it.

The damned thing was so open, with no place to hide anything bigger than a fountain pen. We could wrap the corpse in a bed mat or something and dump it in the back and take it out to the country. But as I pondered this unhopefully, police wagons were cruising back and forth in the side streets in both directions, and we couldn't expect to be lucky for ever.

Anyway, if we bluffed our way out of town in the half-tonner, somebody would remember, and somebody would find the body and put the facts together. I took it for granted that somebody would find the body. I thought wildly of films in which two men shouldered a corpse through crowds pretending he was a drunk friend, and got away with it. We wouldn't get away with it. Dai and me on the front seat and a stiff sitting between us didn't seem convincing at all.

I was growing, actually, desperate and hysterical, and I had to slow myself down and try to turn it into an engineering problem, like building a road. But I had never been trained to build a road in secret under the noses of the police force.

I looked up and down the street at the other buildings and thought that if we had a helicopter or a big catapult, we could move the thing to another hotel, or a store, and wash our hands of it. I actually thought seriously about this till I realised I was avoiding the problem and not solving it. But I kept studying the other buildings until I had to think of something.

I went back into the hotel muttering a catapult, a bloody catapult. The hotel was five storeys high and since we lived on the ground floor, I had never investigated higher than that. But there was indeed a lift, an old-fashioned one built to accommodate not more than five persons, and with iron trellis gates. I opened it and got in, and it worked fine. A bloody catapult, I muttered, and then forcibly stopped myself from muttering. At the top floor I got out and left the gate open to immobilise the thing.

It was the roof I wanted. From outside it looked like a flat roof with a parapet, in which case there must be a way up to it without needing a ladder. It now became obvious that the hotel wasn't a simple unified structure, it had been extended once or twice and the top-floor corridor branched off in various directions at various levels. A little winding staircase, I tried not to mutter aloud, a little winding damned blasted staircase.

There were no little winding staircases. I stood and took deep breaths and thought slowly and started exploring the corridors again; very quietly, because it would do no good to disturb a guest and be seen snooping about up there when I lived four floors down.

One of the branch corridors ended in a half-glazed door. It was closed with two bolts, both fairly solid with old paint, but I got them open without too much noise, turned the handle and pulled. It was perfectly immovable. I was sweating freely and panting before I had the inspiration of trying to push instead. The door too was stuck with paint, but it gave outwards fairly easily on to a narrow gallery. And on the narrow gallery there was no winding staircase, but there was an iron ladder bolted into the wall. I climbed far enough to get a look across the roof, and it was flat.

I closed the door without bolting it and took the lift back down. I had just closed it on the ground floor and was going back to my suite when I ran into the barmaid, presumably on her way to the kitchen or the lavatory.

'Were you looking for me, sir?' she asked nervously, and I said:

'No. I mean, yes, I was looking for you, I wanted some matches, but ha ha I discovered I have some.' I patted my pocket, which contained no matches, and smiled gruesomely at her.

'There is a bell in the bar, sir,' she babbled. 'I am going for coffee, if that is all right.'

'Yes, yes, of course, take your time,' I said. I sounded like a boy soprano. She waddled away into the bowels of the hotel, and I went to the suite and gave four knocks. Dai let me in. I closed the door. Somebody knocked on it three times. I opened it.

Malcolm was there, in a nice off-white suit and with a high-ranking uniformed swine at his side. So help me, I've always thought Dai was neurotic about cops, but this place seemed to breed them as a staple industry.

'Sorry to disturb you, John,' Malcolm said, and he was still the brisk strategic commander. He smiled a self-deprecating smile. 'I thought I should get out into the field to see how things are going. You've had an intruder here, I believe. Hello, Dai.'

Malcolm and the officer stepped inside and I perspired at them confidently.

'I don't know,' I said. 'Somebody searched the place while we were out. Police, I suppose.'

Malcolm glanced momentarily at the officer, who clamped his jaw and said, 'We must be thorough.'

'Of course,' Malcolm said.

'Then another policeman arrived,' I said, trying to slow it down and not babble. 'He went out through the courtyard. The french window was open.'

The officer went to the french window and looked round the courtyard.

'It does seem an odd situation for an economic administrator.' Malcolm chuckled. 'Variety is the spice of life. A bit of excitement keeps us young, I suppose.'

'That's certainly one theory.' I forced myself to chuckle too. The officer came back from the french window and opened his palms to indicate that there was nothing there. A man of few words.

' I just thought I should check the report,' Malcolm smiled. 'We don't want any harm to come to *you*.' My smile merged into facial cramp as he put his hand on the door-knob.

'Oh. I'll wash my hands while I have the chance,' Malcolm said, and showed his palms streaked with dust. 'Through the bedroom?'

'The plumbing's wonky,' I said. 'You could use Dai's.' And Dai said, very offhand, 'No, I think they've fixed it.' In any case, Malcolm was doing everything at a brisk executive pace, and he was already at the bedroom door.

Dai sat down and picked his nails. I looked at the officer and he put his hands behind him and looked at me and gave me a tiny smile and looked away and we stood avoiding each other's eyes till Malcolm swept back from the bathroom and said, 'Right!' and strode out to the corridor followed by the officer. I remained standing, and working my face muscles back to life.

'I thought of that too,' Dai said. 'Laughing boy was too damn public, so I put him in the wardrobe.'

'Always meddling with something, aren't you? We'll take him on to the roof. A bloody catapult.'

'You've gone all cryptic, boy, you'll 'ave to unscramble that last message, see?'

'Never mind. Wait here.'

I went out again and scouted the ground floor. Keeping well back, I could see Malcolm and his officer friend in the street outside, conferring and pointing in various directions and giving orders to three understrappers. After a year or so they all moved away. I went back into the suite and we got the body from the wardrobe. I put one of the peaked crash helmets on him and pulled it down at the front and we took him out into the corridor with the movie technique, which was pretty awkward as Dai was a head shorter than me. But we made the lift in safety, and bundled him in and Dai propped him up while I closed the gates and pressed the button. The lift seemed a lot slower this time, but I drew reassurance from Dai because he looked perfectly calm and expectant, as if he was simply helping with a routine job that I had worked out.

Halfway past the third floor the dim light in the lift went out, and the lift stopped. A second later we heard a distant bang.

'Somebody's blown the power station,' I said calmly in the darkness.

'Or something.'

Doors started to open in the corridors and we heard people telling one another that the lights were out.

'They catch on fast in Tatra,' I muttered to Dai.

Below us I could see matches flickering in the corridor, and Dai said, 'Well, we had a good innin's, you can't win 'em all, can you?'

I roared, 'Go back to your rooms, everyone, and lock your doors. The fugitives are armed and dangerous!' A moment of silence and then a babble and a scurrying, and the slamming of doors.

'That was a good trick,' Dai said. 'Now pull a pair of wings out of your sleeve and we're home an' dry, boy.'

'There must be a trapdoor. Get on my shoulders.'

'He's slipping.'

'Let the bastard slip. Come on.' I grabbed him to hurry him up, but found I was addressing the corpse. I felt Dai's groping hands and held them till I got him orientated, then stooped down and got one of his feet in my hands and straightened up. His shoe heels dug into my shoulders.

'I hope you feel like wrigglin' a lot, boy,' he muttered. 'It's built for midgets.' I could hear the creak of the trap and then his feet rose clear of my shoulders and clipped me smartly on one ear. We stopped talking because there was only one way to do the thing and no need to discuss it. I fumbled round and got the body round the waist and hoisted it up, and it wasn't at all pleasant when the face nestled coolly against mine. It is also fantastically difficult to manœuvre a dead body in a small lift, and I didn't think, in fact, that I would be able to raise it high enough. But it suddenly lightened and I realised that Dai was hanging down through the trapdoor and getting a grip on it. I slid my hands lower down and pushed it upwards.

It might stick in the trapdoor, so I didn't push hard, just gave it enough support to let Dai do the manœuvring from above. Some time later the dead feet rose up past my face in the dark and I heard the weight being handled on the roof of the cage.

It wasn't as easy as I had hoped to get myself through the trap. The roof was low enough for me to grab the opening with a jump, but there wasn't enough room simply to swing myself aloft. It was going to be a squeeze, and I hung by my elbows and walked up the cage door while Dai straddled the opening and gripped my shoulders and pulled. I had to stop and drop and take off my jacket and throw it up to Dai and then try again without benefit of shoulder pads.

We did it, and the three of us knelt on the cage roof cosily waiting the next move. I felt Dai's hand groping for me, and putting something in my hand. The tyre lever. I couldn't quite reach up to the locks of the doors above. I felt Dai tapping my shin and trying to lift my foot off the floor. He had crouched on hands and knees, and it was my turn to stand on him. I used the lever as a pick rather than as a jemmy, fiddling to find the latches and lift them, and eventually I got them both, but the closure mechanism evidently didn't depend on electric power and they wanted to close again. I kept my body in the opening and got into the corridor and lay on the floor and took hold of the corpse when Dai hoisted it, and we got it into the corridor.

I didn't want to linger, but I stood for twenty seconds or more to make sure of my bearings. I didn't want to spend half the night staggering up and down corridors carrying a corpse and looking for the exit. The easiest way to carry the burden now was across my shoulders. We got it up there and moved.

I got the door all right with the help of a faint moon glimmer.

'It doesn't pull, it pushes,' I whispered. Dai opened it and I bent and dumped the corpse through it on to the terrace. After the darkness of the interior, it was quite light enough outside to get about confidently. I got the body up the ladder with a fireman's lift, and lay down beside it on the roof with my lungs bursting.

'Nice view,' Dai whispered.

'Did you bring the camera?' I gasped.

'What do we do with the body, if it isn't an obscene answer?' he asked.

'A bloody catapult,' I said. I could sense him shrugging in acceptance of our insanity. We picked up the load and crossed the roof diagonally to the alley that separated the hotel from the building next door. The gap was only about five feet and the other building was a few inches lower than ours. I took the body by the hands and Dai took it by the ankles and we stood on the parapet and started to swing it gently back and forward till we had a nice rhythm going, and then I said, 'One . . . and two . . . and three!' Because of our unequal heights it rose slightly askew, hit the edge of the building opposite and hung half over with the legs sticking out.

'He'll never win the long jump,' Dai muttered. 'He's a dead giveaway, isn't he, the silly old Tat.'

'The idea,' I panted, 'is to get across there and chuck him on to the *next* building. Otherwise they'll twig where he came from.'

'No wings.'

'We can jump.'

Dai looked across the gap and shook his head.

'I can't—I'm not afraid apart from bein' bloody terrified, but I couldn't jump that if I had a tiger at my back and a harem in front, boy, I'm tellin' you honest.'

I believed him. I sat down on the parapet and relaxed and breathed a lot. The noises of cops moving about and doors being hammered came up with unexpected clarity from the streets below, and occasionally the beam of a torch swept up and down. I knew I couldn't do it in a standing jump. I had to go to the back of the hotel to get a run along the parapet. I didn't waste any time about it. I think Dai kept his eyes shut. I landed cleanly enough on the other roof.

Dai watched in misery and shame while I got a hold of the body and dragged it callously across the roof to the far side. The alleyway here was more like ten feet, but the third building was two storeys lower and thank God there was no parapet on the middle roof. I rubbed the sweat off my palms and laid the corpse face up near the edge and got a good grip of the ankles. It was damnably hard to start it moving because my feet slipped on the roof. Finally I took off socks and shoes and felt better.

At first the body was just trailed sluggishly in a circle round me, but I realised that the trick was to move in a complementary circle myself while I was getting it clear of the surface; and luckily it wasn't a very heavy man, probably sixty pounds lighter than myself. I got it whirling splendidly. It would have looked better with roller skates, but it was all right. I let it go. I staggered after it and threw myself violently to the side to scrabble at the roof and not go over.

85

The arc was splendid, but the aim wasn't perfectly calculated, and the roof opposite was tiled. The corpse hit it with a mighty clatter and started to slide till it reached the guttering at the front edge of the building, and there it hovered while I lay with my face against my roof and watched it and whimpered gently. A torch flashed below in the main street, and then another, and then a vehicle braked noisily and a searchlight swung from it. I edged back hastily. The searchlight struck the body, which had one arm and one leg hanging over the guttering, and there were shouts from below. Then a rifle cracked. It didn't seem to hit anything.

Next came a machine-gun. Bullets spurted and whined off the face of the building, and finally the corpse started to jerk like a puppet; and as it jerked it slid very very slowly outward and a dozen bullets hit it fair and square. It appeared to levitate and then dropped into the street, accompanied by a triumphant shout. Bloody good luck to you, I whispered to the machine-gunner, I hope it was your boss. What kind of a country is it where they turn artillery on a perfectly innocent corpse out for a night on the tiles?

I put on my socks and shoes and shambled back to the other side of the roof and Dai just looked at me. He was relieved. I let some more adrenalin pour into the blood and took a running jump. Dai caught me by the shirt and gave me the essential twelve inches by which I was going to miss landfall. I was starting across to the ladder when Dai grabbed me by the arm and said, 'Sh.'

I turned to follow his stare, at the roof opposite.

'What?' I muttered, angry.

'A man.'

'You're crazy.'

He pressed my arm more tightly and whispered, 'In the shadow of the water tank.'

There was certainly a water tank, and in the faint moonlight it cast a shadow. But I couldn't see anything. Dai suddenly reached in his pocket and took out the tyre lever, and put it to his shoulder and aimed it like a rifle. There was a sudden shadowy movement in the shadow and it changed shape.

'What the hell was he doing?' I whispered.

'Just a sightseer, boss.'

7

G ENERAL DAREN spoke on the radio at half past noon. On the way from the hotel in the morning we had seen workmen fastening big loudspeakers to trees and windows in the streets and were happy enough to be leaving them behind, but Papa had a big transistor radio with him at the site, and for this important Tatranian event he was in complete charge. The time of the broadcast was calculated to catch people at lunch rather than put them off their work. Our own men were finding bits of shade to sit in and preparing for a bite and a nap, but Papa skittered among them ordering them to gather round.

'It is our beloved President,' he cried. 'It is our privilege to hear the President, the privilege of *everybody*. You! Come and hear the President.' He was calling to Joseph, our fat Boka fan, and wasn't pleased at all when Joseph shrugged and cocked an apathetic ear without moving any nearer. Papa turned on the set and deafened us with the Tatra National Anthem.

'What does he want them to do then, stand to bloody attention?' Dai wondered.

'No,' I suggested. 'Form a line and march into the loudspeaker.'

In fact, Papa himself was standing to attention with his eyes now closed in ecstasy. The music was followed by a fanfare and then a stirring voice which said, 'People of Tatra! Our president!'

The voice that followed was clipped, baritone and as flat as old beer.

'Fellow-citizens.' It also had a mannerism of long pauses that should have been pregnant but were just long. 'I speak to you all today to tell you ... that Tatra ... is still proud ... and free.

'Last night our enemies attacked Victoria. These evil persons, with the help of anarchistic governments abroad, hoped to disturb the order and discipline of our beloved country.

'They failed. Our gallant soldiers and policemen have served Tatra well. One brave detective officer was shot to death by the terrorists ...'

We didn't look at each other. We looked solemn and respectful. We didn't snigger.

'Damage was done to the electricity supply of Victoria. It is repaired.'

'It bloody well ain't,' Dai muttered.

'The ringleaders have been killed or captured by the brave work of our government forces. The crisis is over. You may go peacefully about your work. With the help of Almighty God Tatra will continue to advance to her destiny ... proud and free. And disciplined. Without discipline, we are nothing. A man cannot be a man without discipline. An army cannot be an army without discipline. A country cannot be a country without discipline.

'Each of you has his place and his rank in the great tasks that lie ahead of our proud country ...'

It was hot, and it was boring, and I switched off my brain while the President allocated a place to everybody in Tatra, saving the cosiest one for himself, and started to castigate the evil and misguided Tats who rejected the ideal of discipline and order and were trying to undermine the progress of the country, the sanctity of the family and the chastity of Tat womanhood.

89

'Fat chance,' Dai said bitterly.

'We shall protect you from these evil and subversive elements,' the President thundered feebly. 'We know them, and their punishment shall be just but severe. Help us to help you. Give every assistance to your gallant police force and your proud army. God save Tatra!'

The National Anthem. Under the menacing glare of little Papa the men got to their feet; some of them enthusiastically, a few apathetically. Even Joseph humoured him by nearly shuffling erect, which I thought was wise of Joseph. You don't fall foul of a little man like Papa if he's in a position to get back at you. As the last crashing chord ended, Papa pushed it a bit far by starting three cheers and embarrassing the hell out of everybody.

'Now!' he cried, 'back to work!' The men looked stunned.

'Cool your old motor down, Papa,' Dai told him. 'I don't blow the whistle for another ten minutes.'

The little man was ecstatic.

'Everybody must work harder,' he cried joyfully. 'We must give our all for our beloved President.'

'We'll give our all when I blow the whistle, boy,' Dai told him. 'If you want to work, have a shovel and let's see you, then.'

There was a burst of sceptical laughter. Papa glared at the men and then returned to sanity and said, 'Nevertheless, we must all work hard for the President.' He jumped into the big truck and started to work furiously at reading a handful of papers.

I found Joseph in the afternoon moving muck in a wheelbarrow, about half as efficiently as Martin but not much more slowly than the average Tat, and I said, as lightly as possible, 'Haven't you been arrested yet?'

'Me, boss? I'm a good boy, I work hard for the President one day a week.'

'How about Boka.'

'Boka lives.'

Papa had left the radio playing in case further inspiration was coming. A news reader was announcing the blueprint for the new proud disciplined Tatra, consisting of a stringent regulation against short skirts and tight trousers which the gallant police force would enforce with the utmost rigour.

'Isn't he in jail yet?' I teased Joseph, and he turned an impossibly innocent face to me, with sweat pouring down it, and said, 'I don't know where Boka is.'

'Go with love, you lazy bastard,' I told him, and he said, 'Yes, boss,' and wheeled away the barrow with three small stones in it.

And that was it. Dai brewed up tea at three o'clock and we had it in the hut and gave the men fifteen minutes off in face of Papa's moral indignation at such laxity. They were working all right, for them, and considering the heat, and Dai knows how hard to drive people and when to ease off.

'It's as if nothing had happened last night,' I said. 'I don't believe it did happen.'

'Whatever you're talkin' about, boy, don't forget the man in the spectators' gallery.'

'An optical illusion.'

'The whole bloody country's an optical illusion but I've heard of people being eaten by mirages. Ah, to hell, you're right, boss, let us cultivate our gardens like old Voltaire and forget about it.'

'Malcolm keeps surprising me,' I said.

'He's like a boy playin' cowboys, isn't he?'

'That's what it is,' I said. 'He's always had a hell of a lot more energy than anybody else.'

'I wouldn't say that.'

'What do you mean?'

'Nothin', nothin'—I know, boy, he's your father figure an' you like him, and he's all right, but I can't get comfortable with a man that don't drink or smoke or talk about women, see? My own old dad was like that, but he was my dad and it didn't matter. Maybe if he had been a bit filthy-minded my mam wouldn't have been such a prosy old bitch.'

'What's Myra like? I haven't really spoken to her.'

'She's all right,' Dai was suddenly abrupt and uninterested. 'For a viscountess or whatever it says in the book. She's got 'er troubles.'

'What troubles?'

'We all got our troubles, haven't we, boy? That's all I mean, I got no time for other people's troubles.'

'We'll blast today.'

'You're the boss.'

Dai thought I had some kind of infatuation about Malcolm, and that was an exaggeration. The father-figure accusation probably had some truth in it—at nineteen most of us like having somebody to look up to, and Malcolm was there at the right time. I was pretty surprised to find him playing cowboys, as Dai put it, but what Dai didn't understand was Malcolm's enthusiasm for anything new or difficult. Certainly it was more than ten years since we had met, and it was natural that I should have progressed out of the stage of respectful adolescence, probably healthy that I should be able to see Malcolm more as a contemporary and probably with faults. But he was still a big man to me, and I reckoned that with a government like Tatra's, a really capable and persuasive man like Malcolm was probably the only hope for the place.

I wanted to blast as soon as possible, partly because it had to be done, and partly to make some inroads into the explosive stock. If we used some right away, nobody could be suspicious if it turned out that some of the stuff was missing. Dai and I did it ourselves, on one of the sizeable overhangs a quarter-mile from the site, to remove the overhang and provide us with good tonnage of stone at one go. We uncoiled the wire back to the site and counted heads and got everybody under cover and I pressed the plunger because I like it. I can nearly understand terrorists' passion for blowing up buildings in preference to pitched battles. With high explosive you get a lot of fun for your money. I found Dai in the hut emptying a cardboard box and stuffing things into his jacket pocket. The pocket had a zip-fastener.

'Detonators,' he said. 'Nobody can do much damage without 'em and I would rather have them where I can feel them, see?'

'You can't get them all in your pockets,' I said, 'but it's a good idea. We'll parcel up the rest and put them in the hotel safe every night, if they've got a safe.'

'I would never have thought of that.'

'University training,' I said, 'you illiterate Taffy.'

'I am an illiterate Taffy.'

The town had lost its air of tension. There were people about the streets and the cafés were open. May be there was a new regulation ordering folk to walk about and look happy after the crisis. Instead of going straight to the Louis, which was rapidly become claustrophobic, we stopped at a place called the Acapulco which looked slicker and promised the possibility of more life.

'And birds,' Dai said.

'In long skirts.'

'That's all right, I've got wide trousers, I can nearly put them on without takin' my socks off first.'

Some of the shops and offices had the Tat flag flying outside to show how nice everything was. We went into the cocktail lounge and it seemed pleasant enough and well filled. I was heartened to see that everybody wasn't in a family party. There were even two girls sitting on bar stools without obvious escorts. Dai sat on the adjacent stool and turned away from them to speak to me and turned back and knocked one of their drinks over.

'I've knocked over your drink,' he said, 'I'm terribly sorry, I'm not usually so clumsy, please let me buy you another.'

'No thank you.' She was about thirty and she didn't mean no thank you, she meant that negotiations had opened, and Dai pulled a bundle of ten-shilling notes from his pocket, not at all flashily but visibly, and peeled off two and called to the barman.

'He must be made to pay,' I said. 'It serves him right.'

'No, really.' Everything was fine. The two girls carefully looked distant and disapproving while Dai ordered four drinks, and was picking up his change when he knocked the first girl's drink over again by swinging on the stool and bolting for the door. This time some of it spilled over her, and that was too much.

'Thank you very much,' she said coldly, and the pair of them got up and stamped away to the ladies' room.

'That was very neat,' I said.

He took in the situation and clucked regretfully and said, 'I didn't even think, I wanted another look at him but he disappeared.'

'Who?'

'The visiting man, the little fella who uses your bathroom.'

'What were you going to do, chat about the weather?'

'Oh God, I never even thought what I was going to do, boss. I could hardly turn him over to the . . .' He glanced round the bar and abandoned the last word. 'I just saw him, like, and I had a friendly interest. Anyway, he ran like a rabbit, boy.'

'He saw you.'

'Yes, it isn't a comfortable thought when you think of it. There's another pair of ugly bits over at that table, they might be grateful for a bit of Welsh coal, I shouldn't wonder.' But he didn't really have his mind on the ugly bits.

8

Iɴ fact, we lived a quiet life and got on with the road. A couple of days later we reported to the bar of the Louis on our way from the site to a bath and met a group of visiting newspapermen and got talking to them. It was almost a surprise to discover that there was a world outside Tatra. A few of them had come direct from England, and some others had been shunted over from the Rome offices of English papers to have a look at the trouble spot. We told them about the road and didn't mention anything else. I found myself remembering how offhand and uninformative Malcolm had been when I first asked him about the Boka slogans, because I heard myself saying exactly the same kind of things when one of the reporters asked me.

'Some teenage fad,' I said. 'Like Kilroy was here.'

'We haven't mixed much with the natives, see,' Dai supported me, 'though I wouldn't be surprised if they was friendly if you make the effort.'

'Is there censorship?' the man asked. He was younger and more excited than the others. Pilkington, I think his name was.

An older, leathery reporter told him, 'They've never had enough news to need censorship. Tatra is the un-newsiest country outside Chile. I was here during the war when they thought the Germans or the Italians might invade, and I had a cranky schoolmarmish news editor who once cabled me, "Are there any news?" I cabled him back, "Not a new."'

'But these colonels are different,' Pilkington insisted earnestly. 'Is it all right to talk here, incidentally?' Charles was back on duty at the bar, with a white face and two fingers bandaged. I raised my hands as if I didn't understand the question. Charles moved to the far end of the bar and washed glasses. 'Look at Greece. Look at de Gaulle.'

'You look at de Gaulle,' the leathery man said, 'I've got a weak stomach.'

Pilkington's ears never accepted anything except serious answers. He said to Dai, as to a local and therefore a serious expert, 'I've read the history of Tatra, of course, I did it on the plane. Are there any racial divisions?'

'Yes, indeed to goodness,' Dai said. 'They are split right down the middle, men on one side and women on the other.'

'I mean between the Tat-Tats and the English Tats,' Pilkington explained, and Dai said:

'Certainly, boy, the English Tats are all in the effing army, seein' as how they own the land and the land takes care of itself and they got to have somethin' to keep them happy an' they got tired of old fretwork an' cock-fightin', see?'

The Pilkington boy wasn't sure whether Dai was joking, and I thought he probably wasn't because he always knows unexpected things.

'Does anybody know Magyar?' Pilkington asked the company. 'There's a place called Briznovina in the north of the island, a swamp where the last Tat rebels drowned in 1862. Somebody told me it got the name from their war-cry as they sank. Do you know Magyar, Alec?' he asked the leathery man, who said:

'No, but I'm willing to be introduced.'

A glance of mutual recognition flashed round from the

leathery man to Dai and me. Pilkington said, 'I mean the Magyar language.'

'I know,' Dai said, 'Briznovina, is that it? It means, "Help, I am sinking in this bloody old swamp".'

'No, I think it's a war-cry,' said Pilkington. 'Are you two going to the party tonight?'

'No,' I said, 'but if you've got women we'll gatecrash.'

'No, the official party,' Pilkington said patiently—the boy had learned a lot of patience in conversations with people who weren't up to his level of sparkling intellect. We hadn't heard about any party, but the invitations were at the reception desk when we went to get our keys and put the detonators in the hotel safe. The do was a reception given by the Officers' Club to President General Daren, 9 p.m., decorations will be worn, carriages at 2 a.m.

'Decorations is good,' I said to Dai. 'The Tat army's never fought a war, have they?'

'No, but you get the Cross of Tatra for not fallin' off your horse during the peasant-sticking season,' he said. 'I wish I had brought my Ovaltiney badge.'

'Check inside the baths and the wardrobes, will you?' I said, 'and throw out any corpses the maids have left.' Actually the suite at the Louis gave me the creeps by this time and I had to laugh at it to exorcise them.

At least we had dinner suits, which was more than poor little Pilkington had. We met him at dinner in the hotel dining room, in the same striped lounge suit he had worn in the bar, and I suspected that he probably didn't own a dinner suit and in any case he had been shot out from his newspaper office so fast that he hadn't stopped to think, he was so overcome with excitement at a foreign assignment.

'I can lend you a linen jacket, boy, and you can cut your tie up and stick it under your collar,' Dai told him.

The boy blushed and said, 'No, I don't believe in class distinctions. Evening suits are an outmoded snobbery.'

'Not 'ere in Tatra they ain't,' Dai said. 'You're welcome if you want it, even it it's a bit loose round the old shoulders, like.'

'It's a matter of principle.'

The boy blushed again and his leathery colleague tried not to look exasperated and Dai patted him on the shoulder and said, 'I like a man of principle, my old mam always said you could tell a man of principle but you couldn't tell him much, down with the aristos, okay.'

'I'm not a Socialist or anything,' the boy explained, in case Dai was an idiot, 'but I don't believe in class distinctions. Am I any better than a peasant? Am I any worse than a president?' Even less accustomed to the climate than we were, and in his thick suit, he was flushed and sweating and pathetic.

'I'm better than a peasant,' the leathery man said. 'They can't hold their drink, I've tried it.'

'I meant,' Pilkington told him, 'as a human being.'

We were collected in two limousines, or at least in an old Humber Snipe and an old Fiat to contain Dai and me and the seven journalists. By a bit of brilliant footwork we got into the other car from Pilkington, and the other reporters, instead of talking shop or discussing the big Tat crisis, spent the journey exchanging horror stories about Pilkington. There is always a Pilkington. I suppose their function is to give other people a common ground of conversation, like bomb stories.

'He's all right, the boy,' Dai insisted, 'his mam let him out too soon, that's all.'

'Ah, get away,' they choanused, and 'Stuff that', and 'He's a Martian'.

'When I see somebody going to a presidential reception in a chalk-stripe suit and a blue shirt,' I said, 'I have seen cold courage.' I meant it. I keep out of trouble, but I can never sneer at anybody who takes it on as a matter of principle. 'Ease up a second, laddie,' I said to Dai, 'your hip bones are doing me.'

The Officer's Club was on the sea, like a superior golf clubhouse based on the design of St Pancras Station, with high walls on the landward side and a lot of lovingly tended lawn. The officers were sporting their decorations. There must have been gallantry awards for billiards and rose-grafting and the three-card trick, as well as for not falling off horses. They looked gorgeous. The ladies wore long ball gowns and no nonsense about obscene thighs or even calves to corrupt the natives, though there were a few areas of mammary pushed up into view. Real Scarlett O'Hara country. Nobody blinked at Pilkington's Burton suit, except Pilkington. An inflated serf took our cards of invitation and shrieked us into the white granite ballroom, where a two-minute march brought us face to face with the entire President himself.

Major Land was with him, flashing his teeth and being pleasant, and Captain Daren, the twit Dai and I had met on the old roadworks. I could see the resemblance. The President was also tall, and thin, but his face bones were heavier and the white whiskers gave them visual nobility. Also present in the handshaking group were Malcolm and Myra. Malcolm was wearing a ribbon with a simple little six-sided cross thing, and just before we got within earshot Dai muttered to me, 'See, he's good at not fallin' off horses too.'

The President held on to my hand a little longer than routine required, and said, 'Welcome, Mr Carlyle, you bring us brains and skill and we are grateful.' I looked at him for signs of the ruthless dictator and didn't see any. His speech sounded rehearsed, and badly delivered, and he didn't seem like anything worse than a silly old man.

Malcolm beamed on hearing his words, and I had the disloyal suspicion that Malcolm had written them. Out of the corner of my eye I saw Dai shaking the old boy's hand firmly and bowing slightly from the waist, to an angle that he had probably calculated to avoid disrespect while betraying no servility. Waiters instantly plied us with alcohol from golden trays, and Malcolm slipped over to my side and said, 'This is a change from peasant weddings, eh?'

I smiled. Dammit, I knew why Dai couldn't take to Malcolm, but I liked him and that was all there was to it. 'The President is up to the ears,' Malcolm muttered, 'and I don't know if I've much time for socialising, but it's good to see you. Will you keep an eye out for Myra? Dance with her?'

'Yes, sure.'

'Good man.' He patted my arm and returned to the General's side.

It was not a stingy party. The waiters worked relentlessly to get everybody stoned, and there was a permanent cold table in the adjoining room, and a big bar where everything was free. But the people who knew one another tended to coagulate and not mix with others, and we gravitated very soon to the bar with the journalists where everybody took the mickey out of Pilkington till there was a commotion in the main hall and everybody stood up. The President was leaving. The octet struck up the National Anthem, and I could see young Pilkington wrestling with his principles before he stood up. He wasn't unlike Dai in a way, bolshie by temperament but without Dai's sense of the absurd. As he hesitated, I saw a beefy young lieutenant glaring at him, and was glad that the boy had decided to be conformist.

Malcolm left with the General. I saw Myra standing alone and said to Dai, 'I must try to dance with Myra, she's on her tod. Will you give her a whirl as well?'

'I'm not on duty twenty-four hours a day,' he said surlily. 'All right, I'll give you a hand.'

The band started playing a slow foxtrot, no modern teenage breakthroughs, and I saw her still alone and smiling vaguely with nobody to smile to, so I left the bar and found my way to her and held out my hands. She fell into my arms and said, 'I didn't really think I would, yes it's very kind of you, are you still enjoying Tatra? It's so much warmer than home, but it does cool down mercifully in the evenings. How is the road coming along?' She didn't dance very well. I always thought that the English aristocracy were drilled through foxhunting and dancing and slanging servants from birth. And she didn't wait for answers, she set out to make conversation solo.

She trembled, too. I nodded and grunted when it seemed essential. When the dance finished I said, 'Would you like to come into the bar? Or sit somewhere else?' I was horribly and inescapably stuck with her.

She shook her head and then fluttered her hands and said, 'Nothing, really, John, thank you very much, it was a super dance.' I smiled and offered her a cigarette and she shook her head apologetically and I spent a long time lighting a cigarette while she watched me with eager interest.

Then Dai mercifully joined us and said, 'May I have a dance, Myra? Lady Wreford? Lady Myra?—I'm sorry, I got it all mixed up still.'

She laughed, quite merrily for her, and didn't provide the answer. The music started, and Dai took her on to the floor and I went back to the bar, where I could watch the dancers and not be involved. I lost Dai and Myra and tuned into a conversation about great newspaper expenses swindles, but a few minutes later I caught sight of the gallant Dai and Malcolm's wife, Myra three or four inches taller than Dai and half the thickness. She evidently didn't find it necessary to charm him with conversation, she was simply dancing. In fact, with Dai she looked quite like a good dancer, and her mouth was closed and so were her eyes. Dai wasn't speaking either.

I relieved him a couple of times and found her rather more relaxed but still determined to recognise my class superiority by having conversation with me. At eleven o'clock she came to and told me she must go home. I protested politely and offered to get a car for her, but she had her own car. She insisted on leaving me to enjoy the evening with my friends, and whisked away. I went back to the bar and told Dai, and he said:

'I can stop wearing the old feet out, then, can I?' There was a lot of noise in the place, as there usually is when the drinks flow free, and Pilkington had disappeared.

Dai and I saw him simultaneously, at the bar talking to two officers, and the leathery man, who was with us, said, 'He's getting local colour. He *works*. He behaves like a reporter. Faugh.'

'He's a good boy, a good mam's boy,' Dai said. 'Go to the ant, thou sluggard, my mam always said, consider his ways and dig a little hole in the ground.'

One of the officers was Captain Daren, and the other was the beefy young lieutenant. Pilkington was getting on well with them, they laughed a lot. I turned away from them and concentrated on a long-deferred drink. But Dai kept looking in their direction, so I turned round again. The place was well filled, and people kept moving about, so I could catch glimpses of the trio at intervals. But I realised why Dai was watching. In the first place he didn't like officers, and in the second place the two officers were having too much entertainment out of their conversation. Young Daren produced a long gold cigarette case and offered young Pilkington a cigarette, and the boy, hot and doubtless a bit drunk, and with his egalitarian principles shot to hell, took it eagerly. Daren then snapped a gold cigarette lighter into flame, and Pilkington focussed on it woozily and bent forward to take a light; and Daren gently kept moving the light away from the cigarette and downwards, and Pilkington owlishly followed it till he was bending fully over. And at the same time the beefy lieutenant casually lifted a jug of ice water from the bar.

Dai was out of his seat with his teeth gritted, but a little wall of people passed in front and we heard the shocked wail of Pilkington and the delighted laughter of the two officers; and when the crowd parted Pilkington was standing, trying to be dignified and accept the witty joke, and dabbing at his hair and his suit with a wet handkerchief. I held up a hand, and Dai saw it and smiled and nodded and sat down.

One of the other reporters started to ask me about labour conditions in Tatra, and I told him what I could, and then realised that Dai was no longer with us. I knew where the little bastard would be. Corpses in baths weren't enough for him, he had to keep thinking about justice and the brotherhood of man.

I got up at once and started to edge towards the bar.

It wasn't only Daren and his beefy lieutenant; they were merely the performers. Half a dozen other officers, including Major Land, were hunched along the bar, either enjoying the show or mildly disapproving of it or tolerating it as a traditional officer-and-gentleman sport. And Dai was smiling and smirking at Daren, and swaying slightly, ready to be the victim. There was nothing I could do.

The cigarettes came out and Dai got one into his mouth at the third attempt. Daren almost tittered. The lighter flicked on. What was the harm in it? It was probably a ritual practised on every young officer who joined the club, and not only on foreign civilians. Dai bent and swayed towards the flame. It slowly moved away, but he didn't bend any further and there was a little pause. Another officer laughed hysterically. The beefy lieutenant accepted a full water jug from the efficient barman, and then Dai bent a few degrees further down, and his right hand came out like a cobra and grabbed Daren's wrist and yanked the flame up and he puffed once and swung round to the left, suddenly owlish and drunk again, and the water jug flew into the lieutenant's face and emptied.

'Sorry,' he said drunkenly. 'Were you drinking that?' I had a glimpse of young Pilkington's face in the crowd, with his mouth working nervously; and of Daren's face with trouble on it; and the beefy lieutenant ready for murder.

Both Major Land and I moved, in a nice synchrony really, neither of us appearing to have done anything sudden. I was standing beside Dai and the Major was standing between Dai and Daren. The Major and I were the bulkiest people in the group, and I wondered for a second if it was going to be a slugging match between him and me. But young Daren threw the Major aside with one arm and said, 'A clever little man!'

The Major accepted the attack without being ruffled and said, 'That was a very amusing accident, wasn't it, Paul?'

This was to the beefy lieutenant, and the last word was sharp and superior-officer, and the Lieutenant swallowed and gasped and tried to laugh and said, 'Yes, Major, ha ha.'

'A clever little man, eh?' Daren was blotchy and gone, and Dai smiled drunkenly at him and puffed the cigarette. Daren flicked a glance at me and decided to stick to Dai. The other officers at the bar tried to turn away politely while not missing anything.

'He's trying to make a fool of an officer,' Daren said thinly. A lot of venom the boy could get into a sentence.

Dai smiled at him still and said, 'Sorry, what happened?'

'He needs a thrashing,' Daren said. Dai kept smiling, but

the drunkenness passed from his face and the smile was like a wolf.

The Major took Daren's arm, very hard in his big hand, and said quietly, 'Louis!'

After a second Daren heard the tone and tried to think rationally, and after another second he made an effort at a superior smile and said to Dai:

'You're a stupid common little man, go back and dance attendance on Lady Horseface.'

Dai said, quite amiably, 'I think I will go away, I never did enjoy listenin' to a noisy shit.'

Before Major Land could stop him, Daren had swung his open palm and landed it on Dai's cheek. I was surprised. Dai could have ducked it without even thinking.

'Do you fight duels here?' Dai asked in simple curiosity.

'Louis, that's enough.' The Major had a good grip of Daren again. 'We have all had too much to drink.'

'That shit has,' Dai said, joyfully. 'Peasants can never hold their liquor.'

'I think we'll go home,' I said, and Major Land nodded at me. Both he and I were trying to keep manœuvring to create a barrier, but young Daren wasn't in the mood to be pacified and Dai was not going to be deprived of some trouble.

'The choice of weapons is mine, innit?' he said innocently. 'I choose fifteen-pound hammers.'

'You won't smile,' Daren choked at him.

'Listen,' Dai said. 'Why don't we all step outside—no,' he added to Major Land, 'not for trouble, I only want to show you somethin', see?'

Land kept a tight grip on Daren's arm and said smoothly, 'It's certainly very public here, isn't it? We can have a talk in the gymnasium.' And he glanced at the eager faces of the other officers now frankly staring and added, 'We four. That is all.'

106

Daren was disappointed, but Dai shrugged and fell jauntily in behind the Major and Daren as they walked out of the bar, into the hall, and downstairs. I followed him, cursing quietly.

Land switched on the lights of the gym and locked the door and said, 'Gentlemen, we have come here to say we're sorry and then forget this foolishness. It is no time for private scandals.' He sounded very firm and friendly and persuasive, but Dai said, 'Sure, sure, Major, my mam would hate a scandal, I just want to show you something. Hit me, boy!' This was to me. I thought it was foolish and infuriating, but Dai knew I couldn't let him down in front of other people, and as he stood with feet apart and his chin poked out for a punch I went at it with a straight right and almost hoped I would flatten him. He took my fist in his left palm and put a light wrist hold on me and crouched and swung from the hips and I went cleanly over his head and just managed to land easily on the mat.

Land smiled in approval, but said, 'You are well rehearsed, admirable.'

'Okay,' Dai said. 'You hit me, as long as you know how to fall.'

The Major didn't give him time to set up, but Dai ducked this time and came up under him and instead of throwing him, lifted him and turned a couple of times and then courteously put the Major on his feet. The Major laughed.

'You don' happen to have a shootin' gallery, I don't suppose,' Dai said, not even winded. 'I'll show you some tricks with mirrors an' blindfold shootin'. I don't like swords much, though, I got a delicate skin.'

'I think we've all enjoyed the exercise,' said the Major. 'Now let's go back and have a drink.'

'Did you imagine I was proposing to fight this lout?' Daren asked wildly. 'It's a thrashing he needs.' And, by God, he had his uniform belt off and in his hand and he was swinging it; and it got Dai across the shoulders, once. The Major made to grab Daren, but I grabbed the Major instead and shook my head.

'So be it,' he said.

Dai wasn't there when the young idiot swung the belt again. The third time it swung, his hand was waiting for it. He jerked and let go, and as Daren stumbled forward, Dai was behind him to plant a savage kick on the Captain's rump. Daren fell and picked himself up and rushed. Dai parried him like a matador, spun him round and kicked again.

The fifth kick sent Daren crashing into the wooden wall bars, and he stood up half stunned and snarled at the Major, 'Arrest him! Arrest him! He'll be charged with assault.'

'No, Louis.'

'I'll call the police myself.'

Land barred his way to the door, and being a lot bigger and heavier, he wasn't going to be pushed aside.

'Behave yourself,' he said. 'If you make a fuss everybody will know what a fool you've made of yourself.'

'Who will tell them?'

'I will.'

Beaten, Daren turned to Dai and said, 'I'll kill you.' Then he unlocked the door and left.

'Sorry about that,' I said.

Land was no longer amiable. He closed his face and said, 'You well might be sorry. The officers' corps doesn't take easily to insults.'

'Have they tried forcin' themselves?' Dai asked him. Land walked out without answering. Dai said to me, 'Boy, I could do with a woman, isn't that curious, boy?'

'You could do with a pill.'

'No, I'll have the woman, she can have the pill.'

9

I WAS sure we were in for trouble, and I told Dai to start being nice and servile to everybody he spoke to, even including the workers. We had a mild drinking session with some of the reporters when we went back to the Louis, but we both stuck to the story that Dai's little triumph with the cigarette and water-jug had been a drunken accident, and we crushed Pilkington's attempts to make it a big tale. The leathery reporter, whose name was Alec Thomson, warned me about making enemies of the officers' corps.

'They don't amount to much as a world military force,' he admitted, 'but they've got Tatra sewn up like a drum—always, even before Daren took power. The Army is the Tat substitute for a peerage, they're the old English and French families who walked over the original Tats and took the land and abolished the language. Daren's only a front, of course, but the Army is tough enough to keep right on top on the island.'

'A front? Who for?'

'Nobody in particular. Money. Tatra Mines.'

'Tatra Mines are owned by the government.'

'The government's got half the equity,' Thomson said. 'Forty-nine or fifty-one per cent, it doesn't matter. But the dough is Belgian, or American. Maybe both. Tatra couldn't finance all this new dockyard building and roads and the crushing plant with a tax on maize. It's bauxite money that paid for the coup. I hope the investors know how much of it is going into fancy uniforms and staff cars.'

'Fascism is always corrupt,' Pilkington said. 'It's not true that Mussolini made the Italian trains run to time, I read a piece about it in the *Observer*.'

'I know,' Dai said, 'but see, he had movable timetables that adapted themselves to the trains, see?'

'No,' Pilkington said doubtfully, 'it was all propaganda.' We let Pilkington give us a historical lecture on the shortcomings of Fascism.

Next day a closed Land Rover came screaming out to the site at four o'clock with four uniformed thugs who leapt out as if they were going over the top at Mons. The leader blew a whistle and yelled for everybody to line up. I was up on the scree above, taking sights, and Dai was down below driving the slaves. I could see the policemen grabbing workers and shoving them into line, and I did a rapid slide down to the road with my heart hammering. I know people at home who have minor embolisms every time they see a policeman while they're driving a car, from a kind of free-floating guilt mechanism; and the sight of a uniform was beginning to trigger me like that in Tatra.

I arrived on the road just before one of the cops was going to give Dai a shove and start a nuclear war, and I roared at him, 'What the hell do you think you're doing?' That was the fear reaction, and I clenched my fists to stop my forearms from trembling.

The policeman might well have been the same one who tripped on the hotel verandah on our first night in Tatra. He snapped back at me, 'Police business.'

I had a grip of myself now, and I stopped yelling and said, 'Your credentials, please.'

He glowered and slapped his chest and said, 'Police business. You see the uniform.'

'Anybody can steal a uniform,' I said. 'Dai, please go into

the office and telephone the town and check on these men.'
This was simply a device to get Dai out of the way before
any of the plug-uglies was daft enough to get physical
with him. I stepped up to the cop and got in his way and
said, 'May I see your credentials? I'm in charge of government property, I can't be too careful.' As sullen as hell, he
pulled some kind of ticket out of his pocket and I didn't even
bother looking at it.

'What's your trouble, officer?' I asked.

'Rounding up terrorists.'

'A good idea,' I said. 'But I'm building a road for the
President and these are my workers. They have no time
for terrorism.'

'Oh? Maybe. A list of the names!'

'Okay.'

I went into the hut and found Dai cracking his fingers
and said, 'Stay here in case we have to retreat to a strong
point.' He didn't say anything. I got the pay list and went
outside. The cop took it and started to spell out the names
with his finger, while his three mates stood menacingly
beside the frightened line of men, ready to defend themselve
heroically if one of the workers should happen to sneeze on
them. Number One started down the line.

'Name!'

He found the name with some difficulty and passed on.
'Name!'

The sixth name was Martin Hemper, but the kid who
answered to it was not the ukelele-player. The cop glared
at him.

'Place of residence!'

'Briznovina.'

'Papers.'

The boy started to stammer and grope in his pockets,
and the cop waited, smiling, and then said, 'You are a
terrorist.'

'Me?' The kid was almost amused as well as afraid. 'I wouldn't hurt a fly.'

'You are a terrorist.'

'That's stupid!'

The cop rammed his stick into the boy's solar plexus and said, 'Him!' Two of the underlings grabbed the boy and dragged him through the dust to the Land Rover and threw him in the back while he was still gasping for air. I watched and did nothing, for want of anything better to do. The cop worked his way down the line without nailing anybody else. Then he said to me, 'I want to see all papers.'

He marched into the hut and I followed him swiftly and found Dai sitting with an inch-thick bit of bar iron, bending it round the back of his neck, and the cop trying to analyse him and think of something witty to say.

'What papers do you want?' I sounded businesslike. 'My records are the private property of Tatra Mines and the government.'

'I am the government,' he said inanely, and ruffled through papers on the table without understanding any of them. 'You have been guilty of unauthorised use of explosives.'

'Balls,' I said.

'Oh? You want to be tough?'

'I can use any explosives I like,' I said. 'I build roads with explosives, that's why the President invited me here.'

'Don't talk to me about the President, mister,' he said, 'I've got your name.'

'Get on to Sir Malcolm Wreford,' I said to Dai, 'and tell him to get rid of this interference.'

'I don't work for civilians,' the cop said. 'I've got my orders, and you're on my list.'

It did strike me as a hell of a way to run a country if they had to louse up a road building job because a juvenile army officer couldn't drink without being a nuisance. I took it for granted that if I was on some list young Daren had put me on it.

'If you want to know anything about the road do it through the head office,' I said. 'I have no time to be bothered.'

He gave me a shove in the chest and knocked me against the table. I took his throat and smacked his head against the door, conveniently slamming it shut, and held him there and put on pressure.

'Move, or speak,' I said to him, 'and you'll be a cripple for life when I take you out to your men.' He couldn't speak in any case. 'Do you understand?' His head wobbled and his eyes gaped.

'If I have any trouble out of you,' I said quietly, 'I'm going to tell the President that you begged me to have homosexual relations with you. Do you understand?' I'll tell your mates the same thing. Do you understand?' The eyes gaped a bit wider.

'I'm going to loosen my hand,' I said. 'You will then stand to attention and keep your mouth shut. Do you understand?'

The head wobbled and I stopped choking him. He hung against the door and panted.

'Name,' I said.

'Pildar,' he gasped.

'Right. I want to explain something to you, Pildar. If anything unpleasant ever happens to me or my friend while we're in Tatra there will be fifty British bombers here next day to blow you to blue hell, and you, personally, will be hanged. I am in constant radio touch with the British Air Force Intelligence. Do you understand?' He nodded. I didn't give a damn. He was just thick and ignorant enough to swallow anything that came from a man with bigger hands than he had. 'I am going to radio London with the truth about your homosexuality,' I went on, 'so that if they don't hear from me every hour they will telephone the President at once. Do you understand?'

He nodded. His breath was coming back.

'Stand to attention,' I said, quite kindly. He stood.

'Very well,' I said. 'Dismiss. Don't discuss this with anybody or you'll die.'

I opened the door and he tried to straighten up and walk masterfully back to the Land Rover. He didn't speak, though, which was understandable. He merely motioned his men aboard and climbed in and sat looking military while the car did a showy three-point turn and belted back towards town.

'Back to work!' I yelled. I had the shivers again.

'Boy, man, boss,' Dai said, 'I'm supposed to be the wild Welsh Celt, but you've gone and declared war on the bloody old country—we'll be in jail before teatime.'

'I'm tired,' I said. I came into the hut and sat down and breathed jerkily and said, 'I'm tired of damned animals. My God, he'll take it out on that kid, I should have tried to save him.'

'Don't push it too far, you've got yourself fixed for a hangin' already, boy.'

'We're leaving this useless country on the first plane, Dai,' I said. 'Enough is enough.'

'They'll stop us,' he said fatalistically.

'Not with half a dozen journalists here, they're the luckiest thing that's happened, we'll stick close to them from now on till after the big fake trials.'

'Journalists are always gettin' shot too,' he said. 'All right, all right, I'm not complainin', I enjoyed it quite nice, I was only hopin' you might give him a kick or two in the testicles to keep his old memory fresh.'

I went back up the hill and tried to work with sweat pouring down in a steady flow into my eyes.

When we let the men go for the night I hung about,

reluctant to get into the half-tonner, and Dai said, 'No, I know, I don't exactly feel delirious about goin' back to town, too bad there isn't another weddin' somewhere.'

'Liverpool, for instance?'

'Liverpool weddin's are just lovely, boy, don't you knock them.'

'We ought to let somebody know the kid's been arrested,' I said. 'I don't even know his name.'

Dai chewed this idea with some pleasure, possibly wondering if frigid Nefertiti might thaw more at the second try; and as I deduced his thoughts, I realised that I had concealed from myself my own extra incentive. I didn't know what I thought about Boka's sister; probably merely that she was a girl, and any girl was welcome in a celibate situation; but whatever I thought, I had my first sensation of pleasure in many days when I thought we might meet her again.

We arrived at the village just before seven o'clock and started knocking on doors. At once a change in atmosphere was obvious. The wedding feast was no longer on. Nobody knew anything and nobody wanted to know us, and we couldn't blame them. We finally found the mother of the bride, hot from the stove and unwilling to open the low door of the little stucco house.

'We're looking for Boka,' I said.

'Leave Boka alone,' she said. 'I don't know where Boka is.'

'One of his friends has been arrested.'

'And you are going to arrest him too?'

'But we're not policemen, you remember us at the feast.'

'Who knows who is a policeman?' An awful thought struck her and she cried, 'Not Martin, Martin has not been arrested!'

'No, it was the boy who was working in his place. We think his family should know. Or somebody.'

'You want to take some mother bad news! I don't know anything.'

'Don't be a silly old woman, you're too cuddly to be so stickin',' Dai told her contemptuously. 'We're only tryin' to help, see?'

'They may be in Briznovina,' she said, and then clamped her mouth shut.

'Where is that?'

She waved her hand vaguely towards the north and said, 'Twenty miles, thirty miles, I don't know.'

'You're a darlin' and I love you,' Dai said. 'Ask me to your next weddin' then, love.'

She nearly smiled at him as she closed the door. We looked at each other and shrugged why not? and walked back to the site and got the half-tonner out of the compound and drove towards town to find a decent place to branch off the road. Dai located Briznovina on the map, but if there was a road it wasn't marked. We got off the road and headed towards the first village and through it and I put on dipped headlights as the darkness started to crush down. A kid of ten stood right in front of the truck waving his arms and I stopped within a foot of him.

He danced round to the side and said, 'I know where Briznovina is, mister, I'll show you.'

'Away home to your bed,' I said.

'I'm all right,' he said. 'I would rather have a ride in a car than go to bed. I know where Boka is, you can trust me, I'm very secret.'

We drove on rough tracks for ninety minutes. Once I saw headlights approaching in the distance, and I cut down to sidelights and drove off the road and behind a clump of palms and switched off the sidelights and waited till the car passed. We had acquired conspiratorial habits.

It could have been a riot squad, but it was impossible to be sure in the darkness. I let it well away before we backed out and headed for Briznovina again. I was on full beam, and the kid was pointing triumphantly ahead at Briznovina still about a mile away, when I realised that all the visible house lights in the place were going out. We drove into a settlement of perhaps five hundred population and found it a ghost village. The kid took Dai's hand and we walked round knocking doors and got no answers at all. Three of the doors swung open when we knocked, and we poked our heads inside and shouted and the houses seemed completely empty.

'The police,' the kid said cheerfully. 'They think I am the police, ratatatatat.'

'That does make it sociable,' I said. The kid wasn't worried. He let go of Dai's hand and pranced ahead of us into a field and shrilled, 'Boka! Boka Boka Boka! It's Fadel! Bo-o-o-oka! It's Faaaaaaadel!'

This achieved nothing for fifteen minutes, at which time a figure rose out of the maize and said, 'Don't make such a racket, you'll frighten the crickets.'

It was ukelele-playing Martin. After his appearance, voices started to sound all over the landscape and a trek back to the village began.

'You shouldn't drive so loudly,' Martin told me. 'It worries people. Man, it's a drag crawling through the vegetation twice in one night.'

'Your pal's been arrested,' I said brusquely.

'Lucas! Ay ay. Man, that's not good.' He sighed. 'Well, we don't know, death may be beautiful too. Boka he say.'

We didn't see Boka at first, and Martin took me to an old man to introduce him as Lucas's father. He heard the news in a stupor and then said, 'I knew no good could come of it, they don't care about the law or the church and they laugh at the police. Now he's been arrested.' He turned and walked away with tears on his cheeks. People were lingering about in the street, perhaps afraid that they might have to take to the fields again if the police returned to ask questions with their clubs.

A shrill woman wheeled on Martin and cried, 'You can't stay here, you've given us enough trouble. You'll bring a judgment on us!'

'I'll tell Boka,' Martin said easily.

'I spit on Boka!'

'That's your privilege, what's the fun if you can't spit free?'

'I spit on you!' She did.

'That's a whizzbang aim you've got,' Martin said. 'You're right on the button, doll.'

A girl in her teens standing beside the woman, said to her, 'I'm going with Boka!'

'You're a whore! I'll lock you up tonight, madam!'

'For the police to question me?' the girl asked, without emotion. 'I would rather have Boka than the police.'

'Slut! Trollop! Oh my God, what a time we live in!' The woman started to get tearful and the girl kissed her absent-mindedly on the cheek and walked away with us.

We found the desperate Boka gang camped in a broken-down sheep fold a mile from the village, drinking wine and listening to a harmonica playing Stephen Foster of all things. There were a score or more of them now, girls as well as boys, and Boka arrived just after us with his shirt full of apples. I think they were all curious about us, but evidently it was one of the social rules of the scene that it was square to be too interested in anything. Dai told Boka about the boy who had been arrested, and Boka's eyes filled with facile tears. His emotions were too near the skin. I was looking round half-guiltily for the sister, but couldn't see her. A rawboned young fellow knotted his fists and snarled, 'If they try to get me I'll kill three of them first.'

'To kill an animal is to be an animal,' a girl intoned at him, and he snarled:

'They're not even animals.'

'They are what they are, Tim,' Boka said. 'Everybody's possessed of his own devil.'

'It's easy enough for you, you've got no devils,' the other youngster complained, and Boka said calmly:

'I may have bigger devils than you, Tim, I have savages in me. I have to talk to them all the time to keep them quiet.'

'You don't get angry. You should be angry!'

'I get angry.' Boka smiled kindly. 'I eat it. It's no more crazy than eating apples and turning them into brains.'

'All right, all right, all right.' Tim unwillingly quietened down, and then laughed at himself. There was a fire burning and coffee cooking on it, and in the darkness beyond, some couples were absent-mindedly snogging. Dai took Martin's ukelele and tried the tuning and and started to croon 'Cwm Rhondda.' They also had a social rule of listening to music. When he was finished a girl jumped to her feet and kissed him. It was Marie. I certainly wasn't going to fight Dai for her if she fancied him, but I was more relieved than I should have been when she came and sat beside me later.

'Shouldn't you be back in town mixing with the ruling classes?' she asked me.

'Shut your mouth,' I said. She laughed. 'I nearly choked a cop to death already today,' I told her, 'and I'm not taking any lip from you.'

She shook her head over my stupidity. 'You think you're clever, big deal,' she said. 'I don't get you, man, I thought you were human.'

'I was provoked.' Why the hell should I defend myself to this peasant?

'And you're sorry.'

She touched my arm, maybe in sympathy, and I said, 'Dammit, no, it was good for him.'

'Tsk tsk. You should use your energy for living, you're

turning it backwards.' Martin had the ukelele back and Dai was playing the harmonica in the firelight under the stars.

'What's living? This?' I pulled her round by the shoulders and kissed her

'You're shaking,' she said.

'I've had a hard day, baby.' She touched my cheek with her fingers and, damn her, she made me feel sorry for myself.

'Ah, forget it,' I said.

But she got up and pulled my hand and I got up and followed her out of sight and she sat down and said, 'Now do you need a quick roll in the grass?'

I didn't sit down.

'Don't be cute,' I said. 'I'm not asking anybody for anything, don't act like charity.'

'So what's so grotty about charity, man?'

'My system is give and take,' I said.

'Aw, sit down and don't be dignified,' she said. 'It's give and take, but sometimes it's more on one side than the other. What's wrong with that? You need comfort, you and your big tough act, choking a cop—you feel worse than the cop, man, you're hopped up.'

'I like being hopped up.'

'You don't. I'm only trying to help.'

'By God, you work fast.'

'Listen, man, in this island tomorrow doesn't carry a guarantee, so live.'

'Okay,' I said. 'A quick roll suits me.'

I sat down beside her, but I couldn't start this way, I wasn't in charge and I felt stupid. She patted my hand.

'A quick roll is only a way of talking, it can mean anything. With love.'

'Ha. You love everybody.'

'Now we're in the sex war, where's the profit in it? I love everybody, I love you.' She laughed. 'Not war.'

I shook my head at her in the dark, and she grabbed my

face and pulled it against her shoulder and said, 'You're not fooling anybody. Love. Only love.'

I was going to tell her off, but it all melted away and I gave in and let her wrap me like a warm blanket so soothingly that I was nearly surprised later when I found myself fierce and starving and deliriously cloven to her in the warm grass. I shouted with triumph in the end. Or maybe I heard her shouting.

'Now you're better,' she said wickedly.

'Was it Chekov who advised his son never to make love without taking his boots off?'

'He was a fool. I love your boots.'

'I'll give you them.'

'Is the war over, then?'

'Ah, shut up,' I said.

'Will you choke me if I don't?'

'Marie Marie Marie,' I said. She kissed my face all over. I wanted to cry, but I laughed—the same thing, I suppose.

'Will I see you again?' I asked her.

'I hope so. We'll probably go into town for the trials.'

'Don't be crazy.'

'Crazy is best. No, don't move, you're not heavy. It's not late.'

I wanted to ask more about her going into town for the trials, but I forgot about it and when I left to go back to the half-tonner I hadn't mentioned it again.

I telephoned Malcolm in the morning before we left the Louis and told him about the kid Lucas being arrested.

'I wouldn't worry, John,' Malcolm said. 'There's a big dragnet out and it's bound to pick up a lot of people. You can't tell, you don't know these people.'

'I know this kid,' I said, rather sharply. 'He's completely harmless, he's got nothing to do with any terrorists.'

'In that case he won't be convicted. There won't be any kangaroo trial.'

'He'll get beaten up by the cops before he gets that far,' I said. 'Can you not do something?'

'I can advise the authorities. You're exaggerating this beating-up business.'

'I'm not.'

'I know more about Tatra than you do, John. Let's do our jobs and not try to run the government.'

At least there was no mention of my strangling cops, so it was possible that I had actually got away with that. On the way out of town we found an old Austin stuck by the roadside and a man trying to change a wheel. He waved his hands pathetically at us and I stopped the truck. He swung smartly into the back seat and let me glimpse a heavy revolver and jammed it into my spine and said, 'Drive on. I'll kill you if I have to.'

I let the clutch out slowly and two other men jumped out from behind the Austin and got in beside the first one. Dai and I did our telepathic act and I kept driving and Dai sat sill.

'Left,' the gunman said. I turned left, down a side street with a factory wall on one side and waste ground on the other.

'Stop.'

I stopped. They coshed us from behind. It took three clouts to get me right under.

10

IT could have been anywhere. It could have been a cell in a Tatra jail, or a back room at Joe's or a branch line of a cave. There was a stone floor and there was a stone roof and four walls to go with them, and a thick wooden door; and nothing else. There were knot-holes in the door.

When I wakened up I had a calm sense of fatality. We had done so much evasion and involuntary skulduggery in Tatra that it was nearly a relief to have been picked up finally by the local secret service and classified as official enemies of the state. By this time I was, and Dai knew it, as much an enemy of the state as he was.

There were no signs of permanent torture installations, which I would have taken for granted: idealistic Vietnamese water arrangements, British nerve-gas outlets, cultured French electrodes, West Berlin police boots for dentistry purposes, Hungarian contracting manacles, Greek pincers, Parisian surgical broken bottles. Nevertheless, I took it for granted that we were classified as dead people with nothing left in us but a few hours of entertainment for the forces of law and order.

Our hands were tied behind our backs with coarse hemp. In their place I would have done at least as much. With hands free, a prisoner like me, by this time, and Dai at any time, was dangerous. I lay for half an hour or so before Dai came round, and we looked at each other and at our cell, and thought. With rubber-soled boots we had nothing convenient for exerting friction on hemp rope, and there was nothing, not even a stone bench, as a substitute. We both wriggled into more comfortable positions against a wall and went on thinking.

After a while we put our backs together and worked out the best process of rubbing hemp on hemp. There was no long-term advantage in this, but a free hand is a free hand; and since nobody was troubling us, the time had to be filled in somehow. It takes a long time for hemp to rub hemp away, but we had plenty of time. Once you get the first strands of one twist away, it gets easier. In the end the rope on Dai's wrists parted. His face was white, but he still said nothing. He took a length of his broken rope and started sawing at my rope with it.

So much was done. Somewhere else in the prison, or wherever we were, a door slammed. We sat with closed eyes against the wall.

Nobody came to us. We could hear voices. We got up from sitting against the wall and went to the door. I would have thought that my only concern in a situation like this would have been how to get beyond the four prison walls; in fact, I was mentally surveying the map of Tatra and ruling out the airport, and groping for a picture of the little fishing harbours and trying to remember how to operate a lug rig boat, or a Chinese lug, or a square rig, or whatever kind of boat the Tatra fishermen used. It was probably three hundred miles from the north of the island to anywhere, and the Tats would have fast launches at least, with guns; but the sea is a hell of a size, and if we were officially classified as enemies of Tatra the sea was the only way out of the place. I almost took it for granted that we would get clear of our four walls.

It would be a grave embarrassment for Malcolm, I realised, if the police had finally decided that we were subversives; but I couldn't waste too much concern on Malcolm's embarrassment because I had been thinking about Malcolm and what I had thought was that whatever happened Malcolm would always come out with his dignity unimpaired. Being more interested in the broad issues than in romantics or other nuisances, Malcolm would stay on top and keep his big-time job or get a bigger one.

Dai was crouched at a knot-hole and enjoying the view so much that I elbowed him aside and bent to have a look.

There wasn't much, but the room on the other side was also bare and stone-walled, and a man, one of the three who had taken the lift from us, was writing at a wooden table. We took turns in watching but didn't do anything to attract his attention.

The cell had a little window high up under the ceiling. It was hardly more than an air-hole the size of two bricks. We had given it one look and discarded it. While I was having a squint through the knot-hole another man came into the room next door; the one who had drawn the gun on us. I went on thinking. These men, the three who had brought us, were not on the well-fed scale of the average Tat soldier-policeman; but it was possible that plain-clothes men were picked for the ability to read and write rather than by weight. They were either plain-clothes men; or Boka fans? That was too improbable to swallow; or they were some other lot, from the crowd who had stolen the explosives.

The newcomer tossed his mate a packet of cigarettes, which didn't tell us anything. Then he put two bottles of wine and a loaf of bread on the table.

'What about them?' the writing man said, and his chum said, 'Let them starve.' That made him sound like a Tat policeman. The two helped themselves to wine, and smoked. Another man came in, but I could only see a bit of his body and not his face. The writer looked up and said, 'Oh, it's you.' He didn't seem very interested. 'What's your news?'

'The day after tomorrow.' I saw the third man pick up a bottle and presumably swig from it. 'We're going into town.'

'How many?'

'Three hundred? Four hundred? Plenty.'

'Where's Boka now?'

'I left him near Briznovina.'

I had been trying to identify the familiar tone of the newcomer's voice. Now I was sure it was Joseph, the fat boy from Boka's mob. Dai shoved at me to give him a look, and peered through, and turned to me with his eyebrows raised. He had recognised the boy too.

'We've got the two Englishmen in there,' somebody said.

Joseph's voice said, 'Why? The Englishmen? What do we want with them?'

'They saw Harry.'

'So what?'

'They saw Harry where he didn't want to be seen.'

'Have they told the police?'

'It doesn't matter as long as they can't tell who he is.'

'They don't know who Boka is either,' said the writing man, and his friend said:

'We can leave that to Fatty.'

The boy Joseph protested, 'It's got to be done, hasn't it? It wasn't my idea.'

The outer door opened and somebody shouted something I couldn't make out. The writing man stayed where he was. Joseph and the other one went outside and closed the door. They didn't come back. Dai and I waited for a long time, expecting that the remaining man must come in some time at least to feed us, or shoot us, whatever he had in mind; but he didn't. I patted Dai's pocket and started to scratch round the floor to find a bit of loose stone. After a long scratch we lifted a small piece of broken flag.

We put one of the percussion caps on a level bit of stone. Dai got back out of the way and lay down dead. I threw the loose stone down on the cap and swung away at the same time to avoid any flying chips. It made a good loud report. I crouched against the wall with my hands behind my back, and I shouted, 'The window! They've shot us!'

When our jailer drew the bolts and opened the door a crack and poked a revolver through, the air was still sharp with the explosive reek, and I babbled, 'Somebody shot him through the window!'

He cursed and bent over Dai. Dai swung his legs at the same time as I sprang, and the man lurched so that I didn't hit him dead centre; but there was enough impetus to get him going, and I kept going too and got on top of him and grabbed in a hurry. He wasn't as strong as a Tat policeman. I took the revolver from him. He yelled help. I got up and punched him in the midriff and stopped the noise.

Dai took him and laid him down with one arm up his back and a hand over his mouth, and I dived out, fumbling with the revolver. Unlike Dai, I had no high-class experience with revolvers, but I knew they had a safety catch, and I groped about till I found it and moved it. I threw open the outer door and kept well to the side. Nothing happened. I stuck my head round the door, low down, and saw only countryside. I straightened up and went out. There was no sign of anybody.

In the main room was a steep wooden staircase leading to an upstairs room or a loft. I went up without wasting time and fired a shot at nothing on the way up. This might have given warning to anybody upstairs, but, on the other hand, they must have had warning already, and I decided that a bullet flying about would get anybody worried and anxious to keep back.

It was a loft, and it was empty. I went down again and ran round the house, which was merely a stone shack, a miserable farmhouse with a neglected acreage of farm around it. A rutted track led away from it, to nowhere in one direction and nowhere on the other.

I went back inside and told Dai we were alone. We took the jailer to the outer room and sat him in a chair and he got his breath back and looked at us with neither friendship nor fear.

'Who are you?' I asked him. He simply looked at me.

'If we was genuine Tats we would slap you about a bit, boy,' Dai said. 'You should think yourself lucky and be ready to answer a plain question.

Nothing.

'What have you got against us?' I said.

Nothing.

'It's a terrible temptation, isn't it?' Dai said to me. 'I still got a bump like an anthracite treble on my skull, see? It would be only fair to give you one too.'

The man sneered at him.

'Tie him to the chair,' I said, and Dai said:

'A good idea, then it'll be easier to cut 'is feet off without interruption.' He brought the bits of hemp from the cell and made them into a decent length to bind the man. Then Dai and I went out for some fresh air and privacy.

'There's gratitude for you, isn't it?' he said to me. 'After all we done for Boka an' his hippies. They got no sense of social reciprocity, boy.'

'I don't believe it,' I said.

'Boka's put the old charm on you.'

'Maybe he has,' I said. 'But I don't believe it. Guns and coshes and all the rest of it. It doesn't fit that crowd of kids singing folk songs and shouting Go with love.'

'It fits Fatty all right.'

'Do you realise we could be a hundred miles from anywhere?'

'That's all right, we got legs. Let's take a walk.'

'That's a waste of time,' I said. 'I'm looking at the landscape and I don't know it. It's not noon yet, so that direction is probably east. But we could be twenty miles east of Victoria, or twenty miles north. Or fifty. Or a hundred. We'll have to make the man tell us something.'

'He's a stubborn little Tat, boy, I don't think we'll bash anythin' out of him.'

'Neither do I. We'll wear him out.'

We went inside and found an old newspaper and took a piece each and made ourselves comfortable at the table and read, and had some bread and wine and cigarettes. We read the paper very slowly, to make it last, and when it was finished we read it again. We didn't speak. This is very difficult. It must have been more than an hour before the man suddenly said, 'I'm not talking.'

Dai and I looked up in mild surprise, and then returned to re-reading the newspaper. After ten minutes the man said, 'There's nothing you can do.'

This time we didn't even look up. Ten minutes later he said, 'It'll be all over before you can get to town.'

'Go with love,' I said, and went on reading. I took another drink of wine.

The man started to laugh, and I put the paper on the table and put my hands over my ears to concentrate on reading. 'What do you think you can do?' he demanded, a little shrilly.

'We're not plannin' to do anything, see?' Dai told him. 'We like it here, it's nice.'

The man laughed again and shouted, 'When they come back in two...'

'In two, eh...' I looked at him absent-mindedly, and he shut up. I ignored him now.

'He doesn't mean two days,' I said to Dai. 'They're coming back in two hours. We'll pick them off when they get out of the truck and then drive back to town in it.'

'Do you think they're idiots?' the man babbled. 'You're not dealing with kids now.'

'The man's right,' Dai said solemnly. 'We'll have to aim terribly carefully, boy.' He tittered, and plunged the prisoner into misery and rage.

We took him into the cell and bolted the door on him. He was a poor poker-player. His thoughts were vividly printed on his face as we shut him in, and his thoughts were that we were incompetent fools not to gag him. We rested in the other room, with the door open for me to look out and Dai at the window. The dust-cloud of the truck, when it came, was visible over a mile off. I went into the cell and gagged the prisoner and this time he really hated me.

The easiest plan would be to stay indoors and surprise the visitors when they came in. This had the difficulty that if there were several people in the truck, and only one came in, the others might take fright and drive off leaving us still stranded. Our final plan was for Dai to take the revolver, which I certainly didn't want, and get outside among the scrub while I stayed in the farmhouse.

The truck stopped some distance from the house and somebody shouted. I shouted back, 'Uhuh!' and stood beside the half-open door with my nerves pinging. I heard footsteps approaching, and then stopping outside; and then moving again. It took me a moment to realise that the man had got suspicious and moved to the window to look in. I grabbed a chair and pressed myself back against the wall.

'Where are you?' said the voice.

I grunted, 'Inside,' and saw the tip of a pistol showing inside the open window. It slid forward, and I swung the chair like a baseball bat and followed it through the window. One of the legs got me in the chest, but the man was under the chair and I adopted the system of walloping wild with hands and feet as I fell. There was a shot and a bullet smacked against the cottage wall. My man still had the gun and I couldn't get at it, but I got one of his ankles and turned him over on his face and went down on my knees in the small of his back and got a hand down on his right elbow and kept it pressed down. There was another shot.

I looked up, feeling naked and helpless, and saw another man jumping out of the truck and running, and heard another shot and saw his hand flying up and his pistol soaring into the air. Now I put my other hand over and tore the gun from my man's hand and he screamed, in fear probably. I got up and made for the truck. The second man was reeling about, dazed, and shaking his hand, and I didn't even shove him as I passed. Dai was already in the truck and the motor was roaring. I got in beside him and he drove it right off the track and round in a circle and headed it back the way it had come.

We hardly heard the shot, but the truck leaped, and after a couple of seconds Dai said, 'Back tyre.' He kept on going. In ten minutes the tyre had shredded itself out of existence, and then we stopped and got out to change the wheel. I did this while Dai sat about keeping a watch on the road.

Victoria was twenty miles away. We went straight to the police station this time because we felt virtuous. A middle-aged man came irritably to the counter, and for a second I didn't know what to say without sounding crazy.

'We've been kidnapped,' I said.

'What? What's that? What are you talking about?'

'We've been kidnapped. We were held up by a man with a gun and knocked unconscious and kidnapped.'

'Name.'

I gave our names.

'Addresses.'

'The Louis Hotel.'

'Foreigners?'

'English and Welsh.'

'Passports.'

'They're at the hotel.'

'You must carry your passport.' He was petulant rather than menacing. 'I must see your passports.'

'Okay,' I said. 'We'll tell you the story and you can see the passports later.'

'Don't tell me the rules of procedure,' he warned me. 'You will bring your passports.'

'Okay, forget the whole thing,' I said.

We turned to walk out, and he yelped, 'You will bring your passports!'

We went back to the hotel and had a bath and changed.

'Do you think there's a plane today?' Dai wondered, and I said:

'That's a damned good idea.' I went to the reception desk and was told the next plane was in three days. 'It's *kismet*,' I told Dai, and he said:

'*Kismet* backside.'

I saw Thomson in the lounge writing, with a long drink beside him. It looked like a superior way to pass the afternoon, and we went in to talk to him.

'Hello,' he said. 'I'm doing the sun-drenched strife-torn paradise colour piece for the weekend. I don't know why I take so much trouble, the pencil could do it by itself.'

'Are we interrupting?'

'Yes, thank God. Have a drink.'

'We've been kidnapped,' I said.

'Thank God. Hard news. Start at the beginning.'

Dai told him while I got drinks, and Thomson scribbled in shorthand. When I looked at his flying pencil he said, almost apologetically, 'I try to hide it nowadays. Superior journalists on the quality Sundays would think it was Victorian and prole to know shorthand. Or grammar,' he added drily. 'What are the police doing about it?'

'Asking to see our passports before they can take a statement,' I said. He chuckled and nodded.

'Nothing's changed. Colonels can come and go, but dear old Tatra goes on for ever. Who do you think it was—the Boka gang?'

I laughed.

'The Boka gang is a crowd of teenagers singing folk and staging love-ins. I've met them.'

'The birds are great,' Dai added. 'Great, boy.'

'I was born at the wrong time,' Thomson said. 'I wonder whatever happened to Calaman.'

'Never heard of him.'

'No.' Thomson shook his head. 'He would be too old for any dramatics by this time. He was born at the wrong time too. He was the black hope of the underground here during the war. I met him. A hard bastard, but I liked him. His idea was that the Germans or the Italians might invade and set up a quisling government so that Calaman's boys could call themselves the resistance and kill off all the inconvenient people in time for the liberation. He was quite sick when the invasion kept on not coming.'

'Maybe he had a lot of kids,' Dai suggested. 'There's a few hard bastards still alive in the place.'

'Communist?' I asked, and Thomson screwed up his face.

'Communist, democrat, dictator, chancer—I can't see the labels any more, myself. A man like Calaman'll call himself anything as long as he gets to the top. Is General Daren a democrat or a fascist or a republican or what? He's a president, that's what. That's all Calaman wanted, a nice simple undoctrinaire job as God. But he'd be seventy by this time.'

'None of our lot looks more than fifty,' I said. 'Forty's nearer it.'

Thomson wasn't frantically interested, merely nosey like a newspaperman who has seen it all.

'There's got to be an opposition,' he said. 'If it isn't

your Boka man it's somebody else. They could use your Boka man, maybe—remember those gun-happy mercenaries who tried to take over the Paris students' strike?'

'I don't see anybody exploiting Boka,' I said, and Thomson gave me a dry smile and said:

'This bloke's made an impression on you. Tell me about him some time.'

'Any time,' I said. 'I suppose we'd better try the cops again with our cock-and-bull story. Have you got enough for the moment?'

'Sure, sure.' Thomson waved his glass. 'Wreford gave us a press conference this morning. They've got one efficient operator, at least.'

'Yes, he is a right old dynamo, isn't he?' Dai said.

'Mm,' Thomson said. 'He's probably as good as there is, as politicians go.'

The same middle-aged policeman seemed partly pleased that we had obeyed his instructions to bring our passports, and partly peeved that we had had the audacity to stop and get cleaned up in his time. This time he laboriously extracted by questions the entire story which he could have heard five times faster by keeping his mouth shut. When we finished he nodded, and I said:

'What are you going to do about it?'

'I have all the information,' he said importantly. 'Your story will be investigated.'

'Ah, stuff it,' I said. We walked out while he was trying to remember how many laws that remark had broken, and we got into the half-tonner and drove to the site. We were still engineers.

There was nobody there. 'It's Saturday,' Dai reminded me.

'This isn't Liverpool,' I said. 'Saturday is working day for hungry little Tats.' I got on the telephone to Tasker, and he was working at any rate. In fact, his first remark was:

'Perhaps you don't realise that in Tatra we work on Saturday, Mr Carlyle.'

'We were kidnapped,' I said.

'I wasn't joking, Mr Carlyle.'

'Neither was I. We'll make up for it on Monday.'

'Not Monday. Monday is a public holiday. For the trials.'

'Oh yes? Well, it's your road.'

'I have another complaint, Mr Carlyle. I am told you have been employing terrorists.'

'No,' I said. 'You employed them. You picked the men, and I'll mention that to the President.'

'The responsibility is yours.' He sounded both alarmed and bossy, and I said, 'You're a slimy little stoat, Tasker, and I'm coming into the office to screw your ears off.' I wasn't, but I thought the idea might keep him on his toes. In one way, I was sick of the road, but I was sick of the sight of work undone too, and we took out the two movers and played with them for a while. It eased our twisted British consciences.

Malcolm caught us at the hotel while we were wondering whether to spend the evening playing poker with the journalists or hunting for the gay life at the Acapulco. He wanted to speak to us privately.

'The inspector wanted to check your story about this kidnapping,' he said. 'But he agreed that I could probably clear it up more easily. It isn't a joke, is it, John?'

'No,' I said.

'I apologise—but I know your anarchic sense of humour. In that case we'll get a squad out to the farmhouse and see what we can pick up. It's one of the great difficulties about a country with antediluvian communications—outside the town and the big villages, nearly anything can happen.'

'There has to be some place where people can live a natural life,' Dai said.

'Kidnappers?' Malcolm found Dai irritating. 'This must have changed your mind about the Boka gang.'

'It had nothing to do with Boka,' I said, and Malcolm said, as to a stubborn child:

'Everything seems to have something to do with Boka. I know, I know, there's no evidence that he had anything to do with this—maybe. But he's a storm centre, and it's only common sense to get him isolated. We don't even know what he looks like.'

'A very ordinary-lookin' bloke,' Dai said quickly. 'Not that we've had a good look at him except in the dark, see?'

Malcolm looked weary of this subtlety and said, 'You mean you couldn't identify him.'

'I couldn't,' I said.

He looked at me appealing for a renewal of our lifelong trust, and then sighed and said, 'I'd better get back to the courthouse. I've got an all-night job ahead of me.'

He went.

We met Thomson and Pilkington and two of the others in the dining room and talked about Communism and terrorism and other polite subjects and then went to the lounge to play poker and help the journalists to get through their expense accounts. Dai decided to sit the game out and watch and then said he wanted some fresh air, and went for a walk. I got to bed in the small hours, but he was later than I was. I called to him when I heard him coming in, and he came to the connecting door and said, 'I went for a midnight dip, very healthy. Good night.' I knew he hated swimming, but Tatra made me abnormal too.

22

THE Tats were evidently religious people. Bells rang everywhere next morning and the streets were crowded with people in best black; even more of them than usual Thomson told me at breakfast, because of the big joyous holiday next day to celebrate the trials of the terrorists. Dai had breakfast in bed and announced that he was staying there till the spirit moved him.

'The cops won't be bashing the citizens on a Sunday,' I said. 'I thought we might explore the town in the afternoon like tourists.'

'Ah, every town is like every other town, boy, and anyway I'm always gettin' into fights and debates when I'm with you, I'll read a book an' seduce one of the chambermaids.'

'You didn't by any chance find a chambermaid last night,' I said, with a trace of envy, but he only said:

'Me? With my chapel conscience and my old mam always lookin' down at me?'

In the afternoon, after church, the cafés and boozers opened and I had a picture of what Tatra might have been like before the military government, or before the other government, or some time in the golden age when they had governments that didn't work. There were family parties at pavement tables drinking lemonade and eating ice-cream and actual kids playing about and annoying one another, and dogs here and there lying in the sun and dying happily of heat. I found the courthouse, another Palladian-Colonial piece, with forty acres of lawn and trees running down from the front steps to the sea; a nice place for a public park where merrymaking Tats could sunbathe with the majesty of the law scowling down at them.

There were young children here too, but most of the hundreds squatting or sprawling on the grass were young adults; some of them in Sunday best black and some of them in tee-shirts or bright dresses.

Groups here and there were listening on transistor radios to the endless waltzes poured out by Tatra Radio, and other groups had a guitarist or a concertina-player apathetically making quiet music in the buzzing warmth. The cops hadn't entirely signed off for the Lord's day. Although there were no uniforms visible, the few bulky strollers moving about in the park had the unmistakable set of police, glancing suspiciously at the length of girls' skirts and thinking their own strange private thoughts.

Thomson and Pilkington and I had come this far with no destination in mind, and the sea attracted us and we moved towards it. A young fellow in a hurry bumped into me and we both said sorry and then I recognised him as tubby Joseph. He jerked back in alarm and bolted round a big tree, and I nearly started after him, but then I thought that I wouldn't know what to do with him if I caught him, and I merely stared in the direction he had taken.

'Somebody you know?' Thomson asked sleepily. 'If there's any civilisation left in Tatra there should be a hut place down by the beach selling iced lager.'

'No,' I said, 'he worked for me on the road . . .'

But I slowed up a lot and kept looking. Then I saw Joseph some distance away, because he had a pink shirt that caught the light. I was sure it was him. He was walking among sitting bodies. He stopped. Somebody got up to shake his hand. Thomson and Pilkington had walked on, and I stood with my hand shading my eyes and tried to identify the two distant figures. Unconsciously I started moving towards them.

Joseph, if it was Joseph, patted the other man hastily and trotted away somewhere in a businesslike fashion. And two of the hefty plain-clothes men started to walk through the crowds to where the other man was still standing. I got to within sixty yards of him, and the two policemen reached him just about then. One of them made a grab for him and as I kept walking I knew it was Boka. I saw him smiling and nodding and holding out his hands. One of the policemen grabbed a wrist and twisted it and started to drag him away. Boka went willingly, but with his arm twisted; and I was moving nearer all the time. Marie sprang up from the grass with a hand out, and the other cop grabbed her, and I saw his face and the grin and the square hand twisting her hair, and I knew I was now in desperate trouble because my legs were starting to speed up. I could see Marie in a cell, somewhere far underground and away from the world, and four or five of them, with hands and grins; and I suppose if we hadn't cached our stolen guns in the hotel courtyard I would have shot the policeman dead without taking thought.

But before I could have done that, and long before I could reach him and smash the grin into his throat, a rawboned boy had sprung from the grass and done that for me. The cop released his hold on Marie, and as she stood everybody sprang up round her and there was a sudden movement that hid the policeman from me. The crowd was scattering and somebody was dragging Marie back and as they cleared I saw young Tim with clenched fists and I saw the cop smashing a cosh down on his shoulder and two other cops leaping over sitting people and closing in on him.

My legs stopped running. Other people, scores of them,

were scrambling to their feet and backing away and a long avenue formed up which the three policemen ran, carrying Tim face down and automatically kicking and punching at him while they yanked him up the broad shallow steps of the courthouse and into the darkness beyond. I was standing, foolish, isolated, with the Sunday picnickers backed away from me.

Thomson came up while I was still standing there and took my arm and took me down to the hut place on the beach for an iced lager. I caught him looking at me curiously, but he didn't ask me any questions, and he diverted Pilkington when the boy wanted to instruct us on the differences in police methods between England and the Mediterranean countries. Thomson was a comforting presence, although he didn't talk a lot. He gave me the impression that a man could see a lot of evil and stupidity and still believe that the human race wasn't too terrible, and this was a kind of reassurance that I needed. He also offered me his spare ticket for the trial.

'I would go, anyway, to the public benches,' I said.

He smiled and said, 'You could try if you like. I don't think anybody but the very best people have a hope in hell.'

'I could get a ticket from Malcolm,' I said.

'Fine.'

'No, I'll take yours. Thanks.'

Dai came back to the Louis for dinner, and we told him about the Sunday-afternoon entertainment.

'I'm glad they got Tim,' he said dispassionately. I stared at him and hated him, and he said, 'It's his fight, boy, I don't want you in any trouble. Who would give me a job if you were in a Tat jail? Honest, John, don't get into trouble, we both want to get out of this stinkin' country an' back to some rain and grime and fish and chips. Please.'

'Okay.' He hadn't seen young Tim being dragged away and maybe that was why he could take it so rationally. An

Italian television team arrived on the island in a charter plane and checked in at the Louis, including two good-looking dolls, and after dinner the foreign colony took over the lounge to drink and exchange suggestive talk. I expected Dai to be in like a mole, but after looking over the birds and saying hello to them he said he felt like having a shower and a stroll. I followed him to his suite.

'*You're* not up to anything, are you?' I asked him.

'There's only two birds, see? If I give them the old patter I'll have both and nobody else will have any fun.'

'Where are you going?'

'For a stroll. You're not my bloody keeper, boy.'

His touch of anger angered me and I said, 'I am your bloody keeper, boy, I don't want you in any trouble either.'

'I'm not in any trouble, you can have the Italian bits.' He was standing in the shower soaping furiously under his arms, his gestures almost angry.

'I don't want the Italian bits,' I snapped. 'Where the hell are you going?'

'Leave me alone!'

We were now fighting mad. I couldn't believe it, and neither could Dai. We glared at each other, and I turned away at the same time as he did. I went out into his bedroom, but I couldn't quite go away because I was too worried. He came out towelling himself and avoided looking at me.

'I'm going to see a bird,' he muttered.

'Why didn't you say so?'

He looked at me as if he was only now understanding me. 'Don't you know, boy? It's Myra.'

'My God!' I didn't want to believe this either, and I didn't know whether I was furious or disgusted or astonished or contemptuous, and Dai said:

'Don't say it, John, I didn't want to tell you but my God, boy, I thought you knew, you're not blind, see?'

'When did it happen?'

As I asked the question I thought I knew the answer, and he said, 'The very first minute it came out of her like radar, she needs a man and all she got is a dynamic old administrator an' I hope you're not goin' to hit me because I'll have to hit you back.'

'I'm not going to hit anybody,' I said. 'You could have left her alone.'

He threw the towel across the room and said, 'Okay, boy, there's no use talkin' about it.'

'That's why you didn't like Malcolm?'

'I didn't like him anyway, but that's got nothin' to do with it, I'm not goin' to jump into bed with a woman out of spite, is it?'

'Okay.' I couldn't think of anything else to say. I went to the door and then stopped and said, 'Don't get into any trouble,' and I was surprised to see him shaking his head and hear him saying:

'I'm in it now, John. An' I'm not complainin', see?' he added angrily.

I left him. I was deeply troubled, maybe mostly at my own stupidity. The two Italian birds helped to make the evening agreeable, but I reckoned that they were either not interested in anybody or interested only in the TV cameraman and director who had brought them. I drank enough to put me to sleep and I slept.

THE trial, as Thomson had foreseen, was by ticket only. The Press accommodation was in the two front rows, and I sat in the second and tried to look invisible. There was no jury-box. I had never heard anything about the Tat judicial system, but when three judges came in in robes I decided it was probably modelled on the French rather than the English system. Boka and Tim and three men I had never seen before sat on a bench inside a box with a uniformed guard at each end. At a table in the well of the court were three other men in robes, and Malcolm sat with them, making notes on a sheaf of typewritten papers. We all stood up till the judges sat, and then sat down, and nothing happened for a minute or two. The atmosphere was informal and not rigidly silent. Thomson muttered to me, 'Wreford again. He's there to make sure everything looks good. It's a show trial.' When Malcolm looked up from his papers I moved my head to keep out of his sight.

The presiding judge, having murmured for some time to his colleagues, looked up mildly and said, 'The case is one of high treason, encompassing the lesser charges of sabotage and attempted murder. This court is convened not primarily to punish, but in the first place to ascertain the truth. Proceed.'

One of the three robed men on the floor got up, and Thomson muttered to me, 'Chief examiner.' The man shuffled his papers unhurriedly.

'The accused men,' he said finally, 'are Emil Wert; Francis Gall; Theo Freeland; Timothy Burge; John Boka. The first three named are charged with direct complicity in the lesser charges. All five are charged with either direct or indirect complicity in the lesser charges. All five are charged with direct complicity in the major charge.'

Young Tim had a swollen lip and a bruise above one eye.

'Witnesses will explain how the five men came to be accused. Officer Marne.'

Officer Marne came from the audience and stood at a rail in the well of the court. I hadn't much experience of any kind of law, but I prefer a court where the witnesses are kept outside and don't hear the other evidence.

'Give your evidence, Officer.'

The officer took out notes and read a lengthy piece of jargon about being on duty near the power station and seeing accused Wert in the area and later being knocked down by the blast when explosives were set off at the power station. He investigated and found accused Wert still in the area. He was searched and matches were found in his pocket.

'I had cigarettes too,' Wert said cheerfully. 'But the cop stole them.'

'The accused will not speak except when questioned,' the presiding judge said. 'Were there cigarettes?'

'I don't remember,' said Officer Marne.

Malcolm scribbled something and handed it to a lawyer who handed it to the examiner who read it and then said, 'I understand that modern explosives are set in motion with detonators rather than with matches.'

'He set it off with matches,' said Officer Marne stoutly.

There was a pause, and one of the flanking judges asked Marne, 'Are you expert in explosives? Have you used explosives with matches?'

'Not recently, sir.'

'When?'

'No, I haven't, sir.'

There was a consultation among the judges and the presiding judge said, 'For the moment it seems that the possession of the matches in itself does not necessarily point to guilt.'

The examiner pursed his lips and said, 'It does not point to innocence either, sir.'

'I agree.'

The examiner turned back to Officer Marne and we heard about the prisoner's suspicious attitude and attempt to escape.

'I didn't want to be beaten up,' Wert interrupted.

While the judge glared at Wert, the examiner said, 'Are you in the habit of . . . beating . . . prisoners, Officer?'

'No, sir, it's against regulations. Except in self-defence.' I noticed that Pilkington was writing down everything, while Thomson was making lazy shorthand notes only at intervals. Other officers were called to explain how they had come to the aid of Officer Marne when he was being attacked by the prisoner Wert. One of them said that Wert was known to the police as the associate of undesirable elements in the country.

'Who are these elements?' the judge asked.

'I can't give names, sir,' the officer said. 'Otherwise they would discover that we know about them.'

'There are no names,' Wert shouted. 'I'm an honest citizen.'

'Clearly,' said the examiner, 'it would not be rational for the police to reveal their knowledge of other criminals who have not yet been arrested.'

'Perhaps,' said one of the junior judges, 'the bench could see those names without having them spoken aloud.'

The officer looked flustered and said, 'I'll have to ask my superior officer, sir.'

The presiding judge said, 'The private information of the police force is properly kept private. But it is improper in a court of law to accept statements without supporting evidence. You understand, Officer.'

'Yes, sir.' The officer didn't understand, but the examiner explained that the names had to be brought to court. This witness and the next officer described how the prisoner Wert had boasted in the police station that he and his accomplices would blow up the whole town before they were finished. Wert was repeatedly told by the judge to be quiet. They were still at this when the court stopped for lunch.

Thomson and Pilkington and I went to the Acapulco for something to eat, but the dining room was full and we bought sandwiches and sat in the park outside the courthouse to eat them.

'The police could easily falsify some of that evidence,' Pilkington told us solemnly. 'It's a well-known fact that policemen try to stick together and support each other.'

'Do you think he's guilty?' I asked Thomson, who said:

'It's years since I stopped surmising about anything. He'll be found guilty.'

'And they call that justice,' Pilkington said hotly.

Thomson said mildly, 'Maybe he *is* guilty.'

'Ah, but that's not the point! Justice must not only be done, it must manifestly be seen to be done.'

'I've heard that somewhere before,' Thomson said, and Pilkington blushed and said:

'It's a quotation, actually.'

After lunch the examiner suddenly abandoned Wert and said, 'We are not merely dealing with acts by individuals, but with a large conspiracy to commit treason. The centre of this conspiracy is the prisoner Boka.' Boka smiled at him expectantly, and the examiner said to him, 'Do you admit the charge?'

'I don't understand the charge,' Boka said.

'That you have conspired to overthrow the State!'

'Every State is overthrown in time, or overthrows itself,' Boka said. 'You might as well conspire to bring the autumn rains. They will come in any case without your help.'

'You will answer the questions and not make political speeches,' the examiner snapped at him; and the judge backed him up more mildly by saying:

'When the examiner puts a direct question to you, you will answer it plainly.'

'I will try,' Boka said.

'You do not believe in the government,' the examiner accused him.

'I believe in the government in the sense that I acknowledge that it exists.'

'You are opposed to it.'

'I am not interested in governments.'

'You want to destroy all governments.'

'Governments destroy themselves. I am only interested in living.'

'Other people have to live too.'

'We are in agreement.'

'I am not in agreement with a subversive,' the examiner barked.

'I apologise.'

'Answer the questions plainly,' the judge warned him again.

'You don't believe in God,' the examiner said.

'I don't know what you mean by God.'

'This is a Christian country,' the judge said sternly. It was the first time he had shown any emotion. 'In a Christian country the question is simple.'

'I don't find it simple,' Boka said.

'Answer the question,' the judge said.

'In any country everybody creates his own idea of God,' Boka said. 'I can't believe in all of them.'

Whatever the examiner thought, the audience wasn't on Boka's side. The examiner looked round the court and nodded.

'You don't believe in chastity,' he accused Boka.

'Chastity exists, certainly.'

'But you do not approve of it?' The judge was incredulous.

'I neither approve nor disapprove,' Boka said. 'People must deal with their bodies as they choose.'

The court now gasped and broke into a hubbub. Thomson muttered to me, 'He's just a nut.'

'He's okay,' I said.

'He's fine, but he's just a lovable nut. In Tatra you can lay every virgin in sight, but you've got to believe in chastity.'

The judge was in no hurry to stop the chattering. Finally the examiner, very calm and triumphant, was able to go on.

'Your followers think nothing of despoiling respectable girls of Tatra.'

'I have no followers, I am only a man.'

'Your friends, then,' the judge snapped. 'Do not evade the question!'

'Your friends,' the examiner said, 'think nothing of despoiling respectable young girls of Tatra.' The phrase rolled off his tongue with love.

'Some of my friends *are* girls,' Boka said. Young Tim put his head in his hands. The audience gasped again.

'And what is your relationship with them?' the examiner thundered.

'I love them.'

'You *lust* for them!'

'Love is enough,' Boka said patiently. 'Lust is only an incident.'

'Only an incident! Only an incident! Only an incident!' The examiner swept the repetition round the court. 'And what about the virgins you have corrupted with your abominable teaching?'

'Only hate is a corruption,' Boka said. 'Love is the truth.'

'Love love love.' The examiner was either beside himself or getting ready to go there. 'Love that destroys the home and the gift of virginity and respect for God and teaches your friends to take explosives and attack property and innocent lives—that is your kind of love!'

Boka was watching him, but didn't appear to have listened to the words. He said, 'I'm sorry you're angry.'

'Silence!' said the presiding judge.

The examiner swung his attention to Tim and said, 'What did this man teach you?'

Tim looked up, white, and shook his head and stammered, 'I don't know him.'

'You were with him when he was arrested. You helped him to attack the police!'

'No, honestly, I was just in the park, they had no uniforms on, I thought it was a fight and I was trying to stop it.'

'I tell you again, you were with him, you are one of his subversives!'

'No, I swear, I was only there for a picnic.'

'Aha. And you've never heard of Boka, I suppose.'

Tim looked alarmed, and said, 'I've seen his name on walls.' His pallor brought the reddened lip and the bruised forehead into high relief.

'Were there many people there,' one of the flanking judges asked, 'when the prisoners were arrested?'

'Nearly a thousand, sir,' said the examiner, and then turned to Boka. 'Is this man one of your followers?'

'No.' The voice was patently honest. I wondered if

149

Boka was a habitual liar, but I thought he had more probably resorted to a literal lie—if he had no followers, Tim couldn't be one of his followers.

'Is there evidence,' the presiding judge asked, 'to connect the prisoner Boka with the acts of sabotage?' I could see Tim's relief in having the questioning diverted by the interruption.

'The chain of logic is clear,' the examiner said. 'I will show that the prisoner's political activities were the direct cause of the acts; that they were designed to culminate in the acts; and that but for the swift action of our police and army forces, they would have led to further more terrible acts aimed at the destruction of all law and order in the country and a state of anarchy.'

He let the atmosphere cool down by sitting at the table and going carefully through his brief, even taking time to have a mutter with Malcolm, who shook his head warningly once or twice as he pointed to passages in the brief. Finally the examiner leaned over to one of his colleagues and muttered to him, and Junior got up to take over. He ignored Boka and started on Gall, the second of the strangers.

'You are accused of blowing up a section of the post office in Victoria.'

'I am innocent.'

Junior paid no attention to this.

'What do you know about Boka?'

'He's an anarchist.'

'What evidence have you of that?'

'My brother used to be in his gang. He told me they were going to get rid of the government and take over everything.'

'Is your brother still in the gang?'

'No, he's dead. He was beaten to death.'

'By whom?'

'The gang, I suppose.'

'You suppose?'

'Who else? He had let their secrets out.'

'You are also in the gang.'

'Me? I've never been in a gang.'

The junior went to spend some time over his papers and then said, 'I will call Officer Cassell.'

Officer Cassell was still on the story of his heroic struggle to overpower the guilty Gall when the court closed for the day. Dai wasn't in the Louis when we got back, and the others disappeared to telephone their papers. I telephoned Malcolm's house and found him at home. I wondered if Dai had had to leap out of a bedroom window when he arrived.

'I want to give evidence for Boka,' I told Malcolm.

'Evidence that will help him?'

'I don't know. Character evidence. I don't believe he's a dangerous rebel, he's just a hobo philosopher.'

Malcolm was rather distant.

'What you're saying is that you'll agree that he believes in free love and anarchy. Do you think that would help?'

'But these aren't crimes.'

'They're not what he's charged with either, but they're damaging in this country. And don't be too sure, Tat law is very wide on what constitutes working against the state.'

'Dammit,' I said, 'he's only a woolly-minded radical. Like you and me, remember?'

'He's in a particular situation. Listen, John, I've got no patience with this sentimentality. We may not like everything about the law, but if he's guilty in law he's guilty, and I advise you not to draw any more of the wrong kind of attention to yourself.'

'It embarrasses you.'

'It's you I'm thinking about.'

I hung up to prevent myself from saying that I hoped

Dai was giving Myra twins while we were talking. I had a bath and changed my shirt and socks though I no longer had any entirely fresh outer clothes; and I didn't want to send anything to be cleaned because I wanted to be permanently packed for departure. I went to the bar.

Pilkington, the eager-beaver, had finished his telephoning first and was waiting for somebody to drone at.

'That evidence of Gall's was very damaging, wasn't it?' he said. 'Do you think Boka's a Communist?'

'No, he's an agent of the American C.I.A.'

'Is that official? I know they've got a lot of agents. They have a huge budget, of course. Did you know they were behind the Bay of Pigs invasion?'

'That was actually Paramount Films.'

'No, I think it was the C.I.A. But the Americans recognise the Tatra government.'

'Maybe it was some other initials,' I said, tired of the joke. 'The T.U.C., maybe.'

'No, it couldn't be that, that means the Trades Union Congress. They're quite conservative, actually. Not the G.P.U. No. There's a lot of government agencies the general public doesn't hear about, did you know that?'

I was delighted when a girl came to tell me there was a telephone call for me at the reception desk. It was a girl's voice. Marie.

'Don't mention my name,' she said quickly.

'Why?'

'I don't want anybody to think you're mixed up with us. I want to know about the trial.'

'Now?'

'No, not on the telephone.'

'Come here.'

'I can't, I don't look right for a good hotel.'

'Walk along the street outside and I'll follow you.'

'It'll take me fifteen minutes to get there.'

'Right.'

I slunk past the bar to avoid Pilkington's hawk eyes and walked up and down slowly till I saw her coming, and walked towards her and stopped to light a cigarette and said, 'Go along the alley beside the hotel.' She walked on without looking at me, and after stopping and patting my pockets and looking as if I had forgotten something, I turned and strolled back. I took the chance while turning round of having a good look for spies. I was jumpy. I melted into the alley and found her there and took her round behind the hotel and hoisted her up on to the court-yard wall and followed her over. We went in through the french windows and I drew the curtains before I put on the light.

'Man, get this.' She spoke dispiritedly as she looked round the room. 'Big time.'

'Can I get you a drink?'

'No, I don't. All right, where's the loss?'

There was still some gin and some lemonade. She drank it and coughed and sat down and said, 'I've never been in a good hotel. How is he?'

'He's all right.'

'They'll murder him.'

'Maybe not. Do you want to wash?'

'Does it show? You've got a bath of your own, man.'

'You're welcome.'

She looked in at the bath and said, 'Sure.' Without self-consciousness she took off her clothes and laid them on a chair and went in without closing the door, knelt in the bath and turned on the taps. I went back to the lounge and locked the doors. I went into the bathroom and sat on the edge of the toilet seat and told her every word I could remember about the trial.

'It'll all be in the papers anyway,' I threw in at one point, and she smiled pityingly and shook her head.

'Who's this Gall? I don't get the Gall bit.'

'I don't know. Probably he is a terrorist. I don't even know if his brother *was* beaten to death.'

'Why not? It happens. What's happened to Lucas?'

'I'd forgotten about Lucas.'

'If he isn't in court he's dead, man.'

'I believe you.'

'I hope Tim gets off.'

'So do I. Thomson—he's an English reporter—Thomson says your brother's just a lovable nut.'

'He is.' She stood up and I gave her a bath towel and almost without thinking picked up another and started to dry her back.

'He is a nut,' she said, 'but he's great. He doesn't care, he always says it can't be anything more than an experiment, so live while you're in it and go when you go.'

'What about your parents?'

'Only a mother. She hates us. She wanted him to go into the Church or the Civil Service and bring glory to the family.'

'Do you hate her?'

'People are what they are. She's as happy as she can be enjoying her anger.'

'She's the hero in her own movie.'

Marie nearly smiled and said, 'Boka he say.' We went into the lounge.

'I'll get your clothes,' I said.

'All right. I'm comfortable enough if it doesn't worry you.'

'I like looking at you.'

'Look with love.'

For the first time I myself felt self-conscious, and poured myself a small drink without looking at her. When I did look her eyes were wet and she said, 'Hold me, I'm dying of sadness.'

I put down the drink and put my arms round her and stroked her short hair and she said, 'I know he's right, but I hate them, I hate them, John. I can't help hating them.'

'I hate them too.'

'I can't be as good as him, I would kill them all.'

'Ssh.' I kept on stroking her hair.

After a while I let her go and she sat in a chair and I handed her the rest of her drink. She looked at it miserably. I took her hand and led her into the bedroom and she lay under the sheet while I undressed.

'Now you give and I take,' she said. 'I need.' I nodded and put out the light and got into bed without a trace of greed in me and wrapped her up for comfort. Later we loved each other. Later Dai came in and turned on the light. I had forgotten to lock the connecting door.

'Sorry,' he said.

'It's all right.' We both sat up, wide awake.

'It's all right,' he said, 'I just came in to say hello. Hello.'

'Did you have a good day?' I said, and it sounded so silly that I added, 'I mean it.'

'Yes, a very good day. It's all very perplexin'.'

'It's the lousy times we live in,' Marie said.

'My mam always said as one door closes another door closes an' pretty soon you can't hear nothin' for the slammin' of doors.'

We had big steak dinners served in my lounge for two, and the three of us shared them when the waitress was gone. Marie sat in a shirt and bare feet. Dai brought a bottle from the bar and drank quite a lot of it. He looked at Marie and said, 'You make a man terrible frustrated, sittin' there with a randy old engineer. It's nice at night. I can't make up my mind whether it's nicer at night or durin' the day, see?'

'Any time,' she said. He laughed and went to his room and closed the door.

'For a second there I was terrified you were going to offer to share yourself,' I said to her.

'I like Dai.'

'Who doesn't?'

'Do you think you can have me exclusively?' she asked.

'As long as I have you at all.'

'I'm glad.' I am glad thou art glad he is glad we are glad you are glad they are glad. We got up at six in the morning so that she could sneak out of the hotel, but I said, 'I want you back tonight.'

'So do I, don't crack, man, you've got a deal.'

After she had gone I tried, but I couldn't see how I could keep her, it all looked very difficult. I decided not to think beyond twenty-four hours. I went out and walked the quiet streets till I could buy the *Tatra Times*.

It was a very sober paper with no jazzy headlines or pin-up pictures except one of the General alongside the title. The main page one story was headed TRIAL FOR TREASON: OFFICIAL SUMMARY. They certainly gave it plenty of space, but the first thing that I noticed was that there were no quotation marks on the page. It was all what they would call objective reporting of the facts.

'Emil Wert, Francis Gall, Theo Freeland, Timothy Burge and John Boka were accused of treason, encompassing the lesser charges of sabotage and attempted murder, in the High Court. The first three named were charged with direct complicity in the lesser charges. All five were charged with either direct or indirect complicity in the lesser charges. All five were charged with direct complicity in the major charge. It was reported by Officer Marne and other officers that the prisoner Wert was seen in the area of the power station before and after the act of sabotage and that he acted suspiciously and attacked the police. . . .'

A lot more of this, without any of the merry interjections

by the prisoner. My eye ran down the columns till it picked up the name Boka.

'Boka gave evasive answers to the questions of the examiner and was ordered to answer by the presiding judge. It was stated that he wanted to destroy all governments and that he did not believe in God, and that God was an invention, and the prisoner said that there were many gods and he couldn't believe in them. It was also stated that he did not believe in chastity and that his followers believed in despoiling respectable young girls of Tatra. The prisoner was questioned about the virgins he had corrupted with his teaching and he said that lust was only an incident. . . .'

It surprised me that the lynch mobs of parents and grandparents hadn't already gathered in the streets after reading this. I went back and showed the paper to Thomson, who read it, nodding, and said, 'It makes its point, doesn't it?' Dai greeted me at breakfast as if we had never exchanged an angry word, and I asked him to take over the site for the day.

'If there's a site left in this mad island, certainly,' he said.

There was a mob in the park outside the courthouse, penned back by a line of policemen. When the court convened, the junior examiner carried on with Gall who returned to his earnest assurance that Boka was the head of a murder tong, or whatever. Then the boss took over again and questioned Freeland, who had been arrested at the post office at the same time as Gall. He said that he was an honest shop assistant who had been running because the noise frightened him, and then went on to admit that he had personally known a member of the Boka gang.

'Why did you not report this to the police?'

'I was afraid I would be murdered.'

'What is the name of this young man who was a member of the gang?'

'Lucas Nime.'

'Where is he to be found?'

'In Briznovina.'

A uniformed officer came from the rear of the court and put a note on the lawyers' table. One of the juniors read it and handed it to the chief examiner. He studied it solemnly, and then said to the bench, 'Our police found the body of Lucas Nime here in Victoria during the night. He had been murdered.'

The court staggered and then hissed with horror. Boka looked calmly at the bench and said, 'Lucas Nime was in the custody of the police.'

'You admit that he was one of your gang!' The examiner stuck to the essentials.

'He was a friend.'

'And how did you know he was in the hands of the police?'

'I was told.'

'By whom?'

'A friend.'

The judge stared at Boka and said, 'You will give the name of the man who told you.'

'I have many friends,' Boka said easily. 'And there are plenty of witnesses to his arrest.'

The examiner studied the message again, and with deep dramatic emphasis said, 'I call Officer Rale!'

Officer Rale came to the front and described how he had heard the noise of a fracas in Albert Square at two on the morning of that very day. On investigating he saw a number of young men running away and found the body of Lucas Nime in the street. Death had been caused by repeated blows on the back and chest and head. From this point there was little more to be said.

The chief examiner turned the case over to the bench.

It took the judges about ten minutes to chat among themselves before the presiding judge looked up for silence and got it.

'In the case of the prisoner Timothy Burge it has not been proved according to law that he was an accomplice of the accused Boka or of any of the others. He is undoubtedly guilty of assaulting police officers in the course of their duty. There is the mitigating circumstances that he may not have known at first that they were police officers, though the fact must soon have become clear. It may be that this act was more rash than considered. He is fined one thousand shillings.'

During the small hubbub, I involuntarily reached into my pocket for money. Thomson muttered, 'I'll pay it. I can say I want to interview him. Don't worry, it'll be your money.'

'In the other cases,' said the judge, 'the police evidence has positively associated the prisoners Wert, Gall and Freeland in the acts of explosion. We must hold the view that although these have been described as the lesser offences, they were not ordinary criminal acts committed for gain, but must irresistibly proclaim themselves as expressions of the major charge of treason.

'In the case of the prisoner Boka, the court has not given undue weight to the prisoner's admissions of immorality. Although these are reprehensible and must provoke the disgust of all decent citizens, they are not in themselves major criminal acts. However, the clear admission and supporting evidence of the prisoner's contempt for legal government, of the one attested case and the other clearly established case of murder associated with the group which he formed, all tend to point to guilt. The evidence of his fellow-prisoners, while it might be regarded as suspect from such sources, must nevertheless be examined in the light of the fact that the fellow-prisoners had nothing to gain from incriminating Boka. The accumulation of all the testimony is also irresistible, and Boka must be held guilty on the major charge.

'The prisoners Wert, Gall, Freeland and Boka, therefore being judged guilty each of one or more capital crimes, are sentenced to be executed. This sentence is subject to the confirmation of the President of the State.'

Boka smiled at the audience as they emitted a feral noise of approval and hate. That bit about the virgins had really got them. The judges got up and left, and as soon as they had gone Thomson was pushing his way into the well of the court to get hold of Malcolm. Thomson knew his way about better than I did. I would probably have waved the money at a policeman and been arrested on suspicion of something at once. Malcolm spoke to the chief examiner, and the chief examiner waved to the turnkeys and Tim was brought out of the dock while Thomson scribbled out travellers' cheques.

I left to try to find Marie in the crowd outside and tell her, but this much news had travelled before me. Some people were milling about exchanging garbled stories from the morning paper. Others were drifting away and saying nothing. The drifters tended to be younger than the millers.

I heard her behind me. She said, 'Don't turn round, I'll follow you. I know.'

I didn't want to head for the hotel with her in daylight so I went down towards the beach, and she overtook me.

'I'm sorry,' I said.

'There's no time to be sorry, man, we have to try some action.'

I thought she meant blowing up the prison and rescuing Boka. 'Don't think I wouldn't,' she said warmly. 'I would blow up every one of them along with it. I just want the President to stop the death sentence.'

'Will we drop in and have a chat with him?'

She didn't think that was funny.

'The stupid old corpse doesn't decide anything without

asking Sir Malcolm Wreford, Martin says. Do you know Wreford?'

'I know him.' I didn't sound enthusiastic. 'But I'm beginning to think he would do the opposite of anything I asked him.'

'Hell hell hell.'

There might be a new way of getting at Malcolm, but I didn't go into the details with her. I said I would try, and left her to dodge about for the rest of the afternoon, and I went back to the main streets to look for a taxi to the site.

Dai was overseeing six workers.

'The job's got unpopular, see? I had a few dirty words with Tasker and he doesn't want to know, everything will be better when the excitement is over.'

'What do you bet,' I asked him, 'that every chit we send Tasker is filed away down a sewer and a new set printed? If anybody ever looks at the books they'll find wages paid out for twenty men today.'

'Plus overtime,' said Dai. 'I heard the verdict on the wireless. What a cow of a country.'

'Marie thinks Malcolm will advise the President about commuting the sentences.'

'In that case God help them all,' Dai said.

'Maybe Myra could put pressure on him.'

Dai thought about this and muttered curses.

'You could phone her,' I suggested.

'I can't phone her from here, through Tasker's switchboard, I got to protect her, John.'

'Ah, screw it,' I said. 'We'll pay the men a full day and let them off and get back to town. Do you not want to do it?'

'No, I don't want to ask her, I don't want her to have to ask that bastard anything. But it's got to be done, I suppose.'

The men didn't mind being sent home with full pay. We drove to the pink house and went up to the door.

'It's a change from nippin' over the wall,' Dai muttered. Myra answered the bell herself, and looked momentarily alarmed when she saw Dai, but he said, 'It's all right, love, nothin' to worry about.'

She looked at me to see if I knew, and said, 'I should be ashamed,' and she smiled a radiant smile. 'Come in.'

We went into the long lounge.

'Do you want to see Malcolm? He's here, but only to bathe and change before he goes to a meeting with the President.'

'That'll be the very meeting,' I said. 'You know about the sentences.' She nodded, not understanding fully, and I said, 'There's no sense in going into it, but the whole thing was an obscenity. Boka isn't guilty of anything. Maybe Malcolm could persuade the President to commute the sentence.'

'You could ask him,' she said doubtfully, and Dai said: 'It's no good, love, but *you* might ask him.'

'Me?' She was worried at once.

'Please, love.'

She looked at Dai tremulously and nodded an said, 'Of course, Dai.' We froze at that point as Malcolm swept into the lounge smoothing back his hair and looking for his briefcase.

'Aren't you working at the road?' he asked. 'Oh, is it still a holiday? Sorry, I'm in a rush, boys—Myra will produce some tea or something.'

'It's all right, Malcolm,' I said. 'I came because I hoped you might weigh in with the President to commute Boka's sentence.'

A trace of annoyance flickered over his face and he was already starting to shake his head when Myra said, 'You must, Malcolm.' Her firm manner was a far cry from her old twitchiness. 'I don't know whether he's guilty of something, but you can't let them hang him or shoot him.'

'It's not up to me, Myra.' His tone clearly said let's not ruin our image by arguing in front of the servants.

'The President takes legal advice from you,' she said calmly. 'You told me this wasn't only a trial, it had to be a good public-relations exercise.' I winced.

'You're oversimplifying what I said, Myra. Everything a government does has a public-relations content. That was what I tried to explain.'

'Mercy is good public relations,' I said, though I had tried not to interfere at all.

'To the Tats?' he asked irritably. 'Boka is the most hated man in the country today.' I noticed that Dai was looking out of the window. I don't think he could bear to look at Malcolm.

'You have to think of the island's reputation abroad too,' Myra said.

Malcolm recovered some of his patient poise and said, 'Politics, as I have also said, is the art of the possible. For heaven's sake, John, you must remember that in some ways this is still a primitive country. It may make mistakes, but without a stable government it will simply revert to chaos. You can't make an omelette without breaking eggs. I know that sounds callous, but it's true.'

'I always find,' I said—I couldn't keep out of it after all—'I always find that when somebody talks about omelettes and eggs the eggs he's talking about are other people. He's more of a chef than an egg.'

Myra interrupted by touching his arm and saying 'Try!'

After a hesitation he smiled and said, 'I'll try. Of course I intend to try.'

She held her cheek for him to peck and he swept out, gladly.

'He won't try,' she said calmly, and I said, 'He might,' and she smiled and said, 'Yes of course. He may.'

Dai was still looking out of the window, and I felt unnecessary.

'I'll order some tea,' Myra said, and I said:

'No thanks, really. I'll take a walk. Maybe Dai wants tea.'

'I do,' said Dai, and Myra smiled and said:

'The house is full of servants.'

Dai laughed. 'I'll have to enjoy my tea, then, won't I?'

I left them sitting down like a placid pair of old friends, and I left the half-tonner and walked, half-hoping to find Marie by accident. The streets were still crowded and the cafés were busy. I didn't see Marie, but I met Martin the ukelele-player, and didn't recognise him at first in his old-fashioned dark suit. He smiled sourly when I looked at it and said, 'Some gear, eh? I've gone underground, man.'

'I'm sorry . . .' It was hard to know what to say. 'I'm sorry about everything.'

He shrugged and stopped his face from trembling and said, 'Boka lives.'

'How is Tim?'

'Who knows?'

'Has he gone away?'

'Man, you need a new diode. They picked him up outside the court.'

'What for?' I was outraged.

'They are what they are.'

I didn't say anything about the chance of a reprieve for Boka. I took him for a glass of wine and we sat and hardly said anything. When I went back to Malcolm's I heard Debussy through the open window, and Dai came to answer the door, with a magazine in his hand. Myra only glanced at me and smiled and went on playing when I went into the lounge. I knew Dai liked women, but I decided he was really in trouble this time. Dai went familiarly to the sideboard and poured me a drink and we sat and listened to Myra playing till Malcolm came home. He obviously hadn't expected us to mount a vigil, and he wasn't happy about it. Myra stopped playing and sat still, listening without turning round.

'Sorry,' Malcolm said. 'I managed to get a reprieve for Gall and Freeland. It was the most I could do.'

'Because they came out with all that perjured rubbish in court?' I asked him.

'I won't even answer that, John.' He put down his briefcase and sat down with the weight of the world on his shoulders.

'It's not very good, is it?' Myra asked the piano, and Malcolm rubbed his brow and said:

'You may think the General is inexperienced politically, but his decisions are usually sound at bottom.'

'The General, the General,' Myra said, and turned round. 'He can't help being a stupid peevish old woman, but do you have to be such a bloody little snob?'

There was an interminable silence, and Myra ended it by walking out of the room.

'She's upset,' Malcolm said.

'So am I,' I said.

'So am I!' he snapped at me. 'I'm trying to do a monumental job for this whole country, and this doesn't make it easier. It's not a schoolroom exercise, I have to deal with brute reality, and it doesn't make it easier either when I am warned that my protégés seem to be involved with the terrorists.'

'Who said that?'

'You simply refuse to understand, John, that nothing goes unnoticed here. How do they know you didn't come here in the first place to make contact with the rebels? They know nothing about you except my recommendation. Confound it, even I don't know—I mean, in the legal sense, of my own knowledge, I don't know.'

'We'd better keep away from you, then.' I was sad and sick. 'In case you come under suspicion too.'

I waited for him to protest. He didn't. I went out and Dai followed me. Outside, I said to Dai, 'We'll get the plane tomorrow if there's a seat.'

'Not me, John. She might want to come, but tomorrow is too soon. I'll wait till next week.'

'Okay,' I said. 'I'll wait till next week.'

'Will you? All right. Thanks.'

The radio loudspeakers were still mounted in the streets and they started up at that moment with the National Anthem followed by an announcement that the prisoners Gall and Freeland had been granted a reprieve by the humanity and generosity of the President.

The President had been unable to exercise the prerogative of mercy in the cases of the prisoners Wert and Boka, but he withheld the reprieves with deep sadness and regret and only because the safety and security of his people must remain paramount. The executions would be carried out at the prison tomorrow at nine a.m. Taraa taraa taraa.

'Looks as if they'll have a nice day for it,' said Dai.

13

THERE were some shops open late, and I made her take some money and buy new, dull clothes so that like Martin she could walk in the street without attracting policemen, and also so that she could come in and out of the hotel by the front door instead of climbing walls.

'You look very respectable,' I said dully. 'So stop worrying. I'm the suspicious character now.'

'How?' In spite of her desperation about Boka she was still worried about me.

'It doesn't matter.' I tried to smile at her, and took her into the bar quite brazenly. We met Thomson, alone, and I introduced her simply as Marie.

Thomson casually looked round to make sure nobody was watching or listening and said, 'Do you notice anything different in the streets?'

'The smell of murder,' she said bitterly, and he nodded agreement, but added:

'There's something else coming. The town feels like a bomb with a short fuse.'

'You don't think Boka's going to blow it up, do you?' she demanded.

He chewed this over and said, 'I don't know, I only know what I write in the papers. I don't think Boka matters.' Marie clenched her teeth, and Thomson went on: 'He might be a cover for something else, even if he doesn't know it. I don't *know*. But I'm planning to keep away from windows. I keep seeing people in the streets walking about looking casual, like extras in a bad movie.'

'With the police they've got here, that's the way Tats walk about all the time,' I said, and he nodded and said:

'Maybe you're right. Revolutions *are* like bad movies, all the same. Think of all that heroic stuff about the Ten Days of October in Leningrad. The truth is, it was like a Mack Sennett one-reeler. With no script.'

'I'm tired, John.' Marie was no longer able to make polite conversation. I got up and nodded to Thomson and we went to my bedroom and absent-mindedly undressed and lay down, holding hands. That's all we did, and I suppose we must have slept a little because night came on and the town got quiet.

At six in the morning the bedroom lights went on and we started up. A uniformed man was at the door. He came into the room and said, 'Get dressed and come with us.'

Behind him came another policeman, very young, and an older one whom I recognised as sickly Pildar, whose throat I had played with out at the road site. Pildar yanked the covers off us and enjoyed the spectacle.

There was no point in jumping about. I sat still and so did she.

'What's the matter?' I asked.

The first policeman said, 'There are some questions about payments made to your labourers.'

'Uhuh.' I got out of bed and reached for my trousers and said, 'I'll see you later,' to Marie.

'Prostitution is a crime in Tatra,' Pildar said joyfully. 'Come on.' He grabbed her by the arm and heaved her out of bed, and gripped her as if he was trying to subdue her struggles although she wasn't struggling, and said, 'You can come as you are.'

'Pildar.' The first man commanded without raising his

voice. Pildar looked at him, but kept his hands working. 'Leave her alone.'

'Prostitution is a crime,' Pildar insisted.

The other man looked at Marie, and perhaps he was embarrassed, and he said, 'Put your clothes on.'

Pildar released her and said, 'There's another one.'

'Mr Owen is out at the roadworks,' I said. Loudly. 'And he isn't guilty of anything, any more than I am.'

'Don't shout,' the boss man said reasonably. 'Stay here,' he said to the young cop. He and Pildar went into the sitting room and I heard them trying the handle of the connecting door. After a few seconds they put their boots to the door and it opened. I heard them going through the suite next door, but they came without Dai. I imagine he was up two flights of stairs inside the hotel, or over the wall of the courtyard, and I hoped he had been wearing pyjamas when he heard the noise.

We were ushered out to a car in front of the hotel. The streets were still deserted, but we soon saw a crowd ahead as we approached the prison. I was numb and sick as death. I didn't know how Marie felt because I was between the boss and the young cop in the front seat and she was in the back with Pildar. I thought I might kill Pildar if I ever had a chance, and wondered what Boka would have thought of that.

The crowd were execution-fanciers, of course. They wouldn't see anything behind the twenty-foot wall, but a lot of people like to be near a death as long as it's safe. Two lines of uniformed men kept a passage clear between the crowd up to the prison gate, and another car was already there. The boss cop called over one of the guards and gave him his card, and the guard went to the gate and handed it through a flap. The people in the crowd hopped up and down to get a good look at anybody who was going inside.

The big gates opened. The other car drove through and

we followed it. The prison yard was about three acres of baked earth with a high wall at the front and the usual glum building facing it. We all got out of the cars. Even at this early hour of the morning, there were uniformed men wide awake and all over the place. No gallows. I assumed that this was the prison of execution, but thought they might use a firing squad, if there was anything left of the prisoners to shoot by this time.

Marie and I stood under the surveillance of Pildar and the young policeman while the boss went to talk to other policemen. The people in the other car were a soldier of some kind—all the soldiers looked like officers—and a medium-built civilian with a doctor's bag. The doctor stood casually and looked around the yard, and glanced at me. He was the man who had left the corpse in my bath. I looked straight back at him, and then raised one eyebrow a quarter of an inch and turned away. Then I caught his glance again. Neither of us showed any change in expression, but that in itself was complicity. On top of feeling sick I began to feel tense.

He stood and watched incuriously as Pildar started to shove us towards a door in the main building. Inside was a reception room with a high counter, but the half-dozen officers behind it didn't seem very interested in Pildar's prisoners. He pulled a ledger round and wrote in it and then barked at Marie, 'Name!'

'Mary Fraser,' I said. He punched me on the cheekbone.

'Mary Fraser,' she said.

'Residence?'

'Cambro.'

'Right.'

Another officer took a bunch of keys and came round to the front of the counter and opened a door and Pildar shoved us through. The turnkey opened the third door along the corridor and stood aside for me to go in. As I went in through the door Pildar's boot struck me on the base of the spine. I fell into the cell stunned with pain and heard him saying, 'I'll be back soon.' The door thudded shut.

Another cell door opened. Pildar's voice said, 'Now we'll make *you* comfortable.'

There was silence for several seconds. A voice from the reception room shouted, 'Pildar!'

He didn't answer till his name was called twice again, and then shouted, 'All right, all right!' Then he said, 'Don't go away,' and laughed, and the cell door closed and his footsteps rang along the corridor.

I got myself straightened up and went to the door, but through the grille I could see only the wall and two doors. Voices started to bark orders out in the yard. I said loudly, 'Marie!'

'Yes.'

'Are you all right?'

'I am all right.'

'I'll kill him.'

'He is only an animal.'

The door at the end of the corridor opened and somebody yelled at us to shut up. I stopped talking. I didn't want anybody else coming along to see Marie.

The cell had no furniture except a stone slab. There was a barred window high up in the outer wall. I jumped up and grabbed the bars and lifted myself to see out. The window overlooked the yard. A squad was being rehearsed in marching from the door to the middle of the yard and forming a line. If that wasn't enough, nearly every other uniformed man in sight was in a second squad practising marching and lining up three deep behind the first squad and shouldering arms. They were going to make a big show of it. Beyond and above the prison wall at the faraway end of the yard I could see . . . I dropped down to give my arms a rest.

When I jumped up again I concentrated on the top of the wall at the far end of the yard. Beyond and above it was a platform that looked like the end of a Simon hoist truck, and beside it a tall pine. Two men in overalls were making a leisurely job of fixing three loudspeakers on to the tree. As I watched, they disconnected one and the platform descended out of sight.

I wondered what Dai was doing. Catching an aeroplane, I hoped. And then I realised that I actually hoped he was buying a fifteen-pounder on the black market and rolling it up to the prison gates. I felt intolerably dry. I lay down on the stone slab and tried to relax completely. The drill went on outside. During an interval, Pildar came to the grille on my door and said, 'Where are the British bombers?' I feigned sleep. He went along the corridor and spoke to Marie, but he didn't go in. I couldn't make out what he said.

Perhaps the worst deprivation was not knowing the time. I tried to sleep because there was nothing useful to do. Everything went quiet. Later it started up again. I got up to the window and saw a double file of men coming out of the other part of the prison building. They lined up. Six fell out and marched towards me. They came to attention outside the reception room.

There were noises in a corridor near mine. I dropped down and went to the door but there was nothing to be seen. I went back to the window and hauled myself up.

Two turnkeys and a priest and the doctor and the prisoner Wert came out into the yard. The four others stood back while Wert went forward and stood in the middle of the escort.

The loudspeakers started up. The deafening amplified noise of a single drum beat echoed inside and outside the yard.

I suppose I had had some hope that the men on top of

the Simon hoist were going to detonate the prison. The hoist was no longer there; only the three loudspeakers.

The escort involuntarily fell into slow time in obedience to the drum beat from the radio, and Wert walked with them till he reached the wall. They did a smart manœuvre and marched out of the firing line. Now the firing squad did their bit of drill and got into position. Then the rear ranks followed them and lined up. I had to drop down and flex my arms and fingers just as an officer marched solo to join the firing squad. I leapt back up again.

The doctor was standing outside the reception room, holding his Gladstone bag to his chest, but I didn't think it could be a machine-gun in disguise. I looked back at the wall in the hope of seeing the hoist. There was nothing but loudspeakers beating a drum. Then one of them coughed out something. Whatever it was seemed to hang motionless in the air, because it was coming straight towards me. Then it dropped and I heard a bang and saw smoke erupting in the middle of the firing squad and heard the officer shout 'Fire' and saw him reel about in the smoke.

There was a rattle of gun-fire; and immediately after it a shout from the crowd outside; and then another dull bang and the smoke burst out afresh. I honestly felt sorry that I hadn't thought of this myself. A loudspeaker is a beautiful weapon to anybody with the sense to modify it a bit, and it doesn't even have to be manned or operated with any tricky radio signals because it has a perfectly legitimate electric cable leading to anywhere you like.

There was more scattered rifle-fire out in the yard, but I don't think anybody had identified the loudspeaker as the enemy because everybody but me had been too interested in the main entertainment; so I assumed, without too much dismay, that they were all firing at one another. Three of them staggered out of the smoke cloud and fell and rolled about coughing.

The doctor ran into the reception room, which was too far away for me to hear much; but he must have sounded an alarm because uniformed men dashed out into the yard brandishing pistols. Then one of them turned and dashed back. He couldn't get in. I saw him pounding on the door with the butt of his pistol.

The corridor opened and I heard footsteps, and then other doors being unlocked. I went to the grille and found myself staring at the doctor. He hesitated, and then said, 'Oh well, one good turn deserves another,' and unlocked my door.

I got out into the corridor and said, 'Where did they put Marie?'

'I'm too busy.'

He was for running past me, but I found Marie's cell and said, 'This one.' He had a carbine in one hand keys in the other, and I think he might have shot me, but he grimaced and unlocked Marie's door. I grabbed her and pulled her into the corridor. The doctor unlocked three more doors and unshaven men staggered out of them.

'Guns in the reception room,' he snapped. They ran past us.

'Where's Boka?' I asked him. He opened another door and was working on another, without answering, and I said, 'Where's Boka?'

'Beat it.'

'You saved your own pal,' I snarled. 'You're saving Boka.'

He got the door open and barked, 'Guns in the reception room,' to the two men inside. As they jostled past us, the doctor said, 'You think I did this to save Wert? He's probably dead anyway. So is Boka. We can use a couple of martyrs.'

I belted him one and took the carbine and the keys and opened the next door. When the prisoner dashed for freedom I put the gun to his chest and said, 'Where's Boka?'

'I don't know—maybe the next corridor.' He was

174

skinny and pale and afraid of me, perhaps afraid of anybody.

I said, 'Okay, guns in the reception room.' We bolted for the next corridor shouting Boka and callously running past grilles with other yelling faces.

The tenth door along was ajar. I kicked it open, keeping well back. Boka was leaning on the wall of the cell with his hands in his pockets.

'I was coming out anyway,' he said mildly. Two jailers were in the cell with him. One was lying on the stone slab, rigid, with his eyes open. The other was sitting against the wall in the same condition.

'The revolution's broken out,' I said. 'At least, something's broken out.'

'It will be the same in the end,' he said.

'I'm letting these poor sods out of their cells anyway,' I said angrily, and he nodded and said:

'Nobody should be in a cell.'

I unlocked two doors and then realised I was wasting time, and gave the keys to the second man and told him to unlock the rest. Young Timothy staggered out into the corridor, blinking. Boka and Marie came out of the cell. Timothy's face crumpled up at the sight and he stood with his head bowed. Boka came to him and I realised from the crouched way he was walking that he was probably in pain.

'I'm sorry,' Timothy said, and Boka punched him lightly on the shoulder and said:

'We live, man.'

I started hustling them back towards the reception room. The doctor had come round and was caressing his chin. He wasn't happy. I gave him his gun.

'Nice to see you up and about,' I said. 'Don't try anything with that carbine or I'll wrap it round your head.'

'I've got no time to fight with you,' he said. 'Get a gun and do something useful.'

'We haven't a chance,' I said.

'This is only a diversion.' He was hurrying to the reception room and we followed. Some of the freed prisoners were positioned at the two windows, shooting out into the yard. 'Everything has been only a diversion.'

The loudspeaker—there must have been one of the loudspeakers actually working as a loudspeaker—was still beating its monotonous drum. At that moment the beating stopped and a voice said, 'The terrorists Wert and Boka have been executed.'

Then the National Anthem played. The radio station must have worked out the whole programme to a stopwatch. It wasn't the announcer's fault that the prison end had gone wrong. And in spite of all the activity inside, the crowd outside couldn't have had much idea of any hitch. A shout came up from them, a mixture of cheer and groan. I edged up to a window. The smoke, or gas, was dissipating, but the men who had been caught in it were still lying down or crouching and coughing blindly.

Then there was a roar like distant thunder, and the broken glass in the windows rattled. The doctor nodded triumphantly and said, 'The government palace.'

'Can we get out by the main gate?' I asked.

The answer was the sound of the main gate swinging open and the disgusting spectacle of a truck roaring into the yard full of soldiers. Old Faithful popped off two gas grenades quite near to them as they jumped out of the truck, but they looked as if most of them would survive that. Boka was beside me, shaking his head sadly. I grabbed him and Marie and said, 'Upstairs, anywhere.'

A machine-gun started to chatter. We dived back into the building and looked for a staircase and got up to the fourth storey and found that the corridors there led round into the barracks block, where we might run into anybody but where at least we were away from the shooting for the moment.

Everybody seemed to be below, joining in the fun. My idea was to find a window on the outside wall and vanish through it, but when I found a room facing out, the ground was fifty feet down from it, and the ground was jagged rocks and beach. I decided to try a lower floor, and stopped dead halfway down the stairs when four uniformed men ran past in the corridor below with pistols in their hands. I pushed Boka and Marie and Timothy back upstairs.

A rope would have made everything easy, even if it also left us swinging for long seconds as helpless targets. There were no ropes anywhere.

The biggest room on the floor was a locker room facing in the right direction, but there was still no rope, and I dismissed the crazy notion of tying all our clothes together and shinning down naked. We weren't wearing enough clothes. I jammed a bench against the door from the inside to discourage curiosity and went round the room in a savage temper. Timothy sat down and held his stomach.

'Some damned police force,' I snarled. 'They can't even afford a damned clothes line. Poverty-stricken wogs.'

'They do their best,' Boka said blandly, and I turned my temper on him and said:

'You don't give a damn, do you?'

'I do, honestly. I don't want to get shot.'

'Why are you leaving me to do all the bloody thinking, then?'

'You're better at it than I am.'

'Oh God.'

'Are these any good?' he had found a bundle of hand-cuffs in a locker. Each set had about eight inches of chain, and I looked at them and said:

'Great. That cuts the drop from fifty feet to forty-five feet.'

He shrugged apologetically. Marie looked at me expectantly. Damn her. I tried all the other lockers in the hope that they might have another fifty or sixty sets of handcuffs, but all I found in the unlocked ones was sandwiches. I ate one out of spite.

Besides the lockers there was a long table and several long low benches. I stared at them trying to transmute them into rope.

'Silly swine,' I said. 'Silly swine.' I was talking to myself. 'Gimme the handcuffs,' I said to Boka.

The benches were about a foot high and maybe nine feet long, with solid wood supports at each end and in the middle, and a square-section wooden strengthening piece running along under the seats. I heaved two of them together end to end and snapped two pairs of handcuffs round the adjoining ends between the seats and the strengthening rails. Marie and Boka at once lifted another bench and laid it in line. When we had three shackled together we hoisted the first one and slid it out over the window-sill. When it was projecting seven feet out into the open, its weight jerked the next bench forward and the projecting bench slapped down against the wall below with a ringing sound. I craned out and looked down. There was a narrow window directly below on the third floor, but none below that.

'We'll have to hope there's nobody in the downstairs room,' I said. 'Hurry up.'

There were only five benches. I didn't want to take the fifth away from its position as a door stop. I left it there. When the fourth was ready to be pushed out, I shackled the trailing end of it to a leg of the table, and we manhandled the table right up to the window and raised it from the floor to let the bench hang as straight as possible.

'You first,' I said to Marie. 'If we get split up, we'll meet . . .' I couldn't think where.

'I'm going to the mountains,' Boka said.

'Stuff that, I'm getting off this island,' I said. 'Hurry up,

Marie, grip the wood between your knees as well as your hands. I'll meet you at the docks at midnight. Hell.' She was already shinning down the first bench. 'I don't know where exactly,' I shouted. 'The docks. Hurry.' I pushed Boka out without waiting for her to get to the bottom. As he clambered backwards through the window, grimacing, somebody pounded on the door.

Timothy got up and leaned on the table and said, 'You go, I'll stay here and hold them back.'

'Get out of that window,' I said.

'It's my turn to take a risk,' he said.

'In your condition?' I asked him. 'You'll get us all shot. Get to hell out.'

He felt so weak that I didn't know if he would be able to climb down, but I heaved him across the sill and left him to it. I wanted to jump after him, but I could picture all of us halfway down while somebody leaned out of the window and comfortably shot us dead. I went back to check the bench jammed against the door. The man outside put a bullet through the lock and missed my foot by an inch. The door heaved from a kick. The bench jerked and started to slide. I got in behind the door and rubbed my hands dry and waited. At the next kick the bench slithered across the locker that was holding it and the door flew open. A uniformed man jumped into the room, half-fell over the bench and dashed for the window with his revolver still reeking. He jumped up on to the table to get a look outside and I came behind him at a sprint and took him in the rump with my head. He slid right off the table and sailed out on to the beach beyond the rocks. I swivelled round and slid out and grabbed the top bench and went down without using my knees to slow me. The drop on to the rocks jarred me and twisted an ankle and I fell gasping with the pain.

The policeman was lying in soft sand, and perhaps only

stunned or mildly fractured; or perhaps dead. It was Pildar. I didn't stop to examine him. Marie and Boka and Timothy were bobbing up and down over the rocks and dunes a hundred yards away, and I started to scramble after them. I heard shouts, and rolled behind a rock.

Some of the forces of law and order had found the window and the benches and were arguing about whether to climb down after the fugitives or take the easy route by the staircase. I waited and cursed myself for not having picked up a weapon somewhere. They finally decided on the staircase.

The beach was a jumble of rock and sandhills and scrubby bushes, and a rock ridge ran from where I was crouching to near the water, a long way away. I kept low and scrambled down one side of the ridge till it petered out, and then hauled myself on my stomach along what dips I could find in the sand till I could reach a miserably small bush. The wind was blowing fine sand into my hair and my face. I wriggled down on the seaward side of the bush and frantically scooped up sand over my legs and waist, like a kid burying the old man on Brighton Beach. I couldn't fight and I couldn't run, only play dead or be dead.

They came down and fussed over Pildar and then scattered along the beach in both directions, but they didn't come down towards the water. Others came with a stretcher and took Pildar away. In the direction of the town a pillar of smoke was climbing into the sky and sweeping inland.

I lay and died of thirst and madness through the day, and rotated my foot to keep the damaged ankle mobile. When night came down, the sky over the town was patchy red with fires and there were faint bangs and cracks every few minutes. The prison itself was quiet. Then it went on fire. I thought for a second I had merely seen red sun-reflection in one of the windows, but even as I looked at it I heard the glass bursting, and the red flames whooshed through and licked up the wall. The prison burst into noise again, both shouts and gunfire. I had no idea what anybody was shooting at, but I assumed that it was the usual compulsion —if people have guns handy and something happens, they're always liable to start firing out of sheer excitement.

The roof burst open and illuminated the beach. I started to scramble again. I soon decided that I would never reach the docks without help. I could force myself to accept the pain, but the ankle wouldn't work well enough. I thought I might risk going back to the Louis if I could make it, but the nearest refuge, if it was a refuge, was the pink villa. I found my way up on to the main road and staggered and slunk along it. When I saw cars coming I dropped to the ground and lay there. The third time I almost fell on top of a policeman, lying on his back with a hole in his head.

The iron gates of the villa were locked. I rattled them. Nothing happened. There were no lights in the house. Savagely angry, I rattled them again. A bullet whanged off the wall near me and I dropped again. I wriggled beyond the gateway.

'Dai!' I shouted. I meant to shout Malcolm, but it was help I needed, which meant it was Dai I needed, and his name came out unconsciously.

After a pause I heard the sound of running feet.

'John! Is that you, boy?'

'Who the hell do you think it is, Julie Andrews?'

'To tell the truth I was sort of hopin' it might be Julie Andrews, we was just thinkin' we could do with a bit of singin', see?'

He opened the gate and helped me into the house after he had locked it again. Myra and Malcolm were in the lounge, in the dark.

'John,' she said. 'That's wonderful. Wonderful.'

'It's not bad,' I said. 'What are we all doing?'

'We're getting to blue buggery out of here,' Dai said. 'But there's no aeroplane and there's no steamer, so we'll maybe have to swim, boy.'

'It's foolish.' Malcolm's voice sounded tight and odd. 'We are not moving from here.'

'We'll have to,' Myra said. 'If we can.'

'Everything will be under control by morning.'

'Fat chance,' Dai said. 'It's a real old slaughter in the town, boy, all them respectable people have gone daft kicking cops and playing with lighted matches.'

'Even a new government will have to go on with the development scheme,' Malcolm said vaguely to himself.

'Come on, Malcolm,' I said. 'I don't like it here. We can get out of the country, at least.'

I got up and touched his arm now that I could see him in the dimness. He shook me fiercely away and said, 'No, I'm not moving.' He had the sharp smell of paralysed panic about him.

'I am,' said Myra.

'Good,' said Dai.

'I said I would meet Marie at the docks if I could,' I said.

'That is good thinkin', boss, maybe we can hire a skiff or somethin'. Get some food and drink, Myra.'

She got up and left the room without a word. Malcolm snapped, 'We will all stay here! It's madness to move anywhere.'

We left him like that. I was all for dragging him with us, but he flailed out at me hysterically when I went near him, and I left him alone. The half-tonner was in the drive along with Malcolm's Rover. We loaded a hamper into the truck and unlocked the gates and Dai got behind the wheel and drove fast, with his head down. We went through the town at seventy and got a kaleidoscopic blur of broken windows and little mobs battling among themselves. One bullet clanged on the rear of the truck and three people had to jump for their lives out of our headlights, but we got through.

We slowed down approaching the docks. There were no lights shining, although the buildings were lit by the fires in the town. Suddenly cautious, Dai slowed down and switched off his lights, and at that instant a bullet came through the windscreen.

'You all right?' I whispered.

'Okay. You, Myra?'

'Yes.'

'Out,' I said. 'Behind the truck. I'll get the hamper.'

We got down low, and Dai said, 'Have this as well, I can't carry everything.' He shoved a pistol into my hand. 'We'll wait two minutes and then run to the right.'

'Don't be daft,' I said. 'You get ready to shoot.' I lit a match and threw it up in the air. There was a shot and then another as Dai fired at the enemy. A yelp.

'Now we run,' I said. We ran.

It was impossible to tell whether the docks were being guarded by the police or the rebels, or whether both gangs were sitting in the darkness firing at random. I stumbled into a broken-open crate of bottles, took one and lobbed it into the darkness. When it broke, two people fired at the sound from different directions. I threw another bottle at the same spot and we ran again. We got round a warehouse shed and on to the quayside and stood in shadow and just waited. There was no sign of activity. I walked away from the others and yelled 'Marie! Marie!' and then ducked down and scrambled back.

There was no answer.

We dodged across the quay. There was a mixed collection of boats tied up side by side and we dropped on to the first one for a look.

'We want something fast,' Dai said.

'No. Okay,' I said, 'as fast as we can get, but we want

183

sail. If we start up a motor here we'll be cut in two, the bastards fire at anything, whoever they are.'

The fifth one out was a double-ender, thirty-five feet and low and beamy with a yawl rig and an old petrol-paraffin engine.

'Where are we going?' Myra asked suddenly.

'Away,' I muttered. 'The police are after us, and the rebels don't like me much either. We might make Cyprus with luck. Or get picked up.'

'Can you sail?' Dai asked. 'I don't want to be nosey, but I suddenly wondered.'

'Enough,' I said. I wondered where Marie was, but I set about hoisting the mizzen and a jib, and didn't hurry in the hope that she would suddenly appear on the dock. She didn't. She might have gone to the mountains with Boka, of course.

I was stealing somebody's boat, but I still had enough conscience not to want to ruin several others. When the sails were up and flapping I untied forward and dragged the warps aft and re-tied the two boats on either side. Then I untied aft and got my feet against the starboard boat and started to walk our boat forward and clear. There was just a puff from the starboard side, and she started to edge forward. I tightened sail and lashed the sheets and we heeled just a fraction and got moving.

Ashore, there was a burst of machine-gun fire and a car's headlights swept through the docks. The car stopped on the edge of the quay and the headlights caught the top of the mizzen.

'John! John!' It was Malcolm's voice.

'Put out that light!' I screamed.

The light went out.

'John!'

'Left it a bit late, hasn't he?' Dai said in disgust. 'To hell with him, there's plenty other boats.' Myra didn't say anything. I had to force my hand to swing the tiller. There was another burst of fire from the direction of the car, but aimed away from us. I let the boat jibe and slide back towards the quay and brought her round as she was going to bump the line of moored boats. We snubbed against the bow of one and tried backwards in stays and I loosened the sheets and let the sails flap. Dai leaned out and fed us backwards along the line till the stern touched the quay wall. There was another burst of fire above us.

There was also a crunch and I realised we had been towing a dinghy without noticing it, and had nearly squashed it under the stern. I lay down and dragged it clear.

'Thank God,' said Malcolm's voice. 'They've gone insane. Looting and killing.'

'Jump down and shut up,' I said. After a long pause he lowered himself from the edge of the wall by his hands and I caught him and helped him down. 'Who else have you got there?' I asked him.

'Captain Daren. I think the President's dead.' Malcolm was once more the crisp executive. The Captain's figure appeared dimly above us and he leapt gracefully down with his gun swinging from one hand.

'Right,' he said, 'start the engine.'

'Too noisy,' I said reasonably. 'It'll attract gun-fire.'

'I'm quite accustomed to gun-fire,' he said acidly, and I would have said something unpleasant, but Myra said, 'I'm not,' and the Captain grunted and said, 'Very well, but get under way.'

'Push,' I said softly. 'Push us away from the wall. Get a bloody oar, Dai, and get us clear or we'll be bumping about here all night.'

I limped up the starboard side to shove our bow round off the wind and haul in the jib and lash it. Then I went back astern and took in the mizzen sheet and pointed her nose along the side of the quay wall. It wasn't only for fear of gun-fire I didn't want to start the engine. If Marie shouted I would never hear above the noise of a motor.

'Get some speed up, man, and get away from this damned wall,' the Captain said helpfully.

'Hoist the main if you want more speed,' I said.

'I'm an army officer, not a deckhand,' he snapped.

'And keep your voice down. Can you steer?'

'Any fool can steer a boat.'

'You can't steer,' I said. The wind was now as awkward as it could be, swinging round ahead and bumping us against the wall, but I figured that if I pushed her bow off the wall and came about we wouldn't have enough water to clear the line of moored boats.

'I can steer,' Myra said.

'Thank God for a good education,' I said. 'Keep her like this because if you turn right off the wall you'll be headed. We might get enough power from the main to get some way on and come about.'

'I know,' she whispered. I left her with the tiller and unfurled the main without loosening the sheet, and hauled it up very slowly to keep the rings from rattling too much. I could feel the difference at once. She still bumped, but she was beginning to cream along.

'Everybody duck and bring her about, Myra,' I whispered. I had forgotten my ankle while we were dodging about on the quay, but the pain was killing me. I loosened the jib sheet and ignored it while I pushed the mainsail over, and then ducked under the boom and tightened the jib sheet on the port side. We got round all right and cleared the wall and headed straight for the line of moored boats. I held the port jib sheet in my hand and lay down under the boom and left Myra to it, and when she swung the tiller over I pulled in the other sheet and we were clear and going. Then the wind dropped slightly and we just inched out to sea parallel to the quay and three hundred yards from the far end of it and comfortably positioned to be shelled out of the water by anybody ashore with a brick or a bottle of petrol. But the sails were dark dirty brown and the moon was over the island, so we might be invisible.

'Get away from that quay,' Captain Daren said testily.

'Will you stop talking?' I pleaded. 'You can hear a voice on the water a mile away.' He stopped talking and slapped his thigh instead.

Halfway out we must have moved clear of a wind shadow, because the sails abruptly wakened up and the rigging creaked and the old boat heeled and came to life.

'That's better,' the Captain said, pleased that I had finally obeyed him by making the wind stronger. Then I heard Marie.

'John!' Very short and sharp. Myra looked up at me for orders. I didn't know what to tell her, but I shouted, 'Here!' I screwed up my eyes to peer into the flickering dimness and saw something white waving on the quayside. Then it started to move out towards the end of the quay. A gun barked on shore.

'Inshore,' I said to Myra.

'Jibe?'

'No, just lose way.' She was letting out the mizzen without waiting to be told. I loosed off about four feet of the mainsheet and threw away the jib and we headed towards the quay, but still moving seaward. I could see her now because her figure was clear of the sheds and clear against the red glow from the town.

Dai was standing up amidships squinting along the barrel of his pistol. 'Damn,' he said, and grabbed the gun from Daren and put it to his shoulder. There was another shot from the shore and Dai fired a single shot. Marie had drawn abreast of us.

Myra headed the boat straight for the wall and Daren yelled, 'Get this boat out to sea!'

Marie swerved and went straight for the edge and there was another shot. She flew forward with hands outstretched and struck the water and I let the main go and threw myself forward and face down. I caught her by the hair and we were almost motionless. Myra shouted, 'Pull that rope tight, Dai!'

The boat hung sluggishly as I got Marie's shoulders and dragged her on deck. The mainsail tightened and I reached back with one hand and yanked the jibsheet. We started to move. I was nearly deafened as Dai loosed a burst of fire a yard from my ear. I bent down clear of the boom and dragged Marie astern and into the cockpit.

'Haul in and get upwind,' I said to Myra, and laid Marie on the cockpit floor. Blood was pouring down her left breast and I heard myself sobbing and swearing. I tore her dress away and moaned, 'Water, water, quick.'

'Where?' Malcolm asked.

'In the sea, for God's sake.'

He bent over the side and gave me his hat full of water, and I cursed again and poured it over her. She jerked and her eyes opened. There was a neat dark hole just inside the armpit, and my mind lost its way as I tried to remember exactly where human beings kept their hearts. It was all right, it must be all right. Myra was leaning over me, and I said, 'Stay at that damned tiller, you bitch.'

'You take the tiller,' she said calmly, 'I haven't let it go. It doesn't look too bad.'

I reached back and got the tiller and tried to stay crouched beside them and steer blind, but it was stupid. I eased back and took a hold of the boat and dragged in the main till it groaned and punched up into the wind and into the darkness outside. Daren and Malcolm were sitting in the big cockpit looking at Myra as she wrapped stuff round Marie's shoulder; Malcolm concerned and interested, Daren fuming.

'The salt water's probably good for it, but there's vodka

in the hamper, Dai,' Myra said. 'It's probably all right, John.'

'Is that the prostitute who was arrested with you?' Daren asked.

'I'm busy,' I said. Dai was uncorking the vodka and taking a quick swig before he gave Myra the bottle.

'That was your idea was it, then?' he asked Daren.

'It was hardly worth saving her,' Daren said. 'You're both still under arrest.'

'He's a rare old comic, isn't he?' said Dai.

'You'll be dealt with later,' said Daren. 'Start the engine and head for Carmel.'

'It's only a six-horse,' I said, keeping it all calm and conversational. 'Sail is faster.'

'Isn't sail and engine together faster?'

'A bit. Not worth it,' I said.

'Start the engine and head for Carmel.'

'What's there, then?' Dai asked him. 'The guillotine?'

'Don't exaggerate, Dai,' Malcolm said. 'This can all be cleared up.'

'There is an army detachment at Carmel waiting for my orders,' Daren said.

'They'll wait a hell of a long time,' I told him.

'I am in command of this ship,' Daren told me coldly. 'Don't add mutiny to your crimes, Carlyle. I won't hesitate to shoot you.' He picked up the machine-gun from the cockpit seat. I pushed the tiller over and the boom swung gently inboard and unbalanced him. Dai took the gun out of his hands and tossed it into the cabin.

'I'm in command of this ship,' I said. 'Sit down and shut up or I'll slap you right across the wrist with a knotted towel.'

He didn't lose an ounce of his superiority.

'I am now the President of Tatra,' he said. 'You'll obey my orders or you'll be shot for treason.'

'Ah, this has gone far enough,' I said. 'Take the tiller, Dai. You,' I said to Daren. 'Get out.'

'Get back to your work,' Daren said. 'You. Start the engine.'

Dai took the tiller and remarked airily, 'He takes this old gun business serious, boy, look at him.' Daren was unbuttoning his holster. I took his wrist and squeezed it quite unpleasantly and took out the gun with my other hand and stuck it in my belt while he was squirming. I turned his arm round his back and walked him down to the stern and held him while I pulled the dinghy alongside.

'Get in there,' I said. 'You're damn lucky I'm not making you walk.'

He started to struggle. I pulled him round and slapped his face and turned him round again and put my knee on his back. He fell into the dinghy. I untied the painter. He stood up in the dinghy and shrieked as we slid away from him.

'That wasn't very wise, John,' Malcolm said.

'Oh, shut up, Malcolm,' I said.

'I know you're overwrought,' he said. 'Trying times, trying times, but we come through them if we keep our heads. Wildness doesn't achieve anything.'

'I never said a word, boss,' Dai said.

'I'll go back, of course, when things settle down,' Malcolm said. 'In the meantime I'll probably take up my old work at the Development Agency.'

I couldn't help being impressed by his sheer resilience. Some men are born to lead, to organise, to be at the top, and he was back at the top, in whatever kind of world he lived in. I realised I had never known him at all, the fervent pragmatic young radical teacher with the broad vision and the creative energy who was also this myopic manipulator hoisting himself into boardrooms and titled families with a new set of principles for every situation.

'Will Myra go back?' I asked, and she didn't look up from Marie, and Dai concentrated on steering the boat.

'I don't think so, do you, Myra? It can be difficult. I think you're right about taking a long rest with your people. The estate's in Cheshire,' he told me. 'Beautiful old place.'

'Falling to pieces,' Myra said, and Malcolm laughed indulgently. I knelt down beside her and held Marie's hand and stared into her face, and honestly, it wouldn't be honest to call her beautiful; nose too lumpy, mouth too big, bones too strong. She was breathing steadily and that was enough.

'Who is the girl?' Malcolm asked kindly.

'Just a local,' I said. 'Marie Boka.'

'We might still get in on that sewage contract in—in wherever it was,' said Dai. I suddenly saw the map of England, and a sixty-mile red line running straight from Liverpool to some crumbling baronial hall in Cheshire.

'It's time you settled down, John,' Malcolm said. 'Marry some nice girl and settle down.' I liked that *some nice girl*— a plumber's daughter, it meant to me now, or a canteen waitress, some nice girl well below the rank of Malcolm's wife. I was nearly sorry for the silly sod.

'Dai should settle down too,' Myra said wickedly. It was mean, to talk in code under Malcolm's nose, but I saw Marie's eyelids flicker and I didn't give a damn for Malcolm.

'I will,' Dai said. 'I got this arrangement with a girl—not legal and official-like, but dead permanent, you know?'

'Boka?' Malcolm said. 'She's not a relative of the dead boy, is she?'

'Not dead,' I said. 'Boka lives.' The fact that the phrase now meant something somehow made it hilarious and I started to laugh. Malcolm laughed too, indulgently.

'He was thoroughly dead the last time I heard of him.'

'I know,' I said. 'But Boka lives.'

Dai had started to snigger quietly at the tiller, and he

said, 'Death might be a good old lark for corpses, but it's no good for people. Boka he say.'

Out in the dark water with the night still warm and the old boat slicing happily along, I felt the hysteria taking hold of me. I thought Dai's remark was impossibly funny. I giggled and tittered and gasped out, 'Go with love.'

'Go with love!' Myra had picked up the hysteria too.

'These catch-phrases,' Malcolm smiled and shook his head sympathetically and thought about his next big promotion and the wonderful job he was doing for mankind.